# A SLUGGISH MURDER

## A WILDWOOD WITCH MYSTERY: BOOK 7

ELLE ADAMS

"I did not steal her sunflower seeds!" said my squirrel familiar, Tansy, as she scampered indignantly at my side. "Your mother needs to get herself a hobby."

"Uh-huh," I said. "Is there a reason there's a sunflower seed shell stuck to your tail?"

"I was framed!" She flicked her tail to dislodge the shell, which I suspected had once belonged to my mother's extensive sunflower collection. "Besides, the flowers were dead anyway."

"I'm not going to argue with that."

Tansy scaled the wall of my dad's house while I knocked on the door. Dad answered with a grin on his chubby face and gave me a hug. "I thought you'd be along soon, since your brother's already here."

Ramsey had beaten me here? That made a change. When I spied Tansy's fluffy tail vanish through the open window, I said, "Sorry, Tansy's a little overexcited."

"Oh, you're both welcome here," he said. "The boys love her. Right, Jessica?"

My dad's wife welcomed me with a smile. "Glad you're here, Robin."

"Me too." I followed them into the hallway and spied Tansy scurrying around, her tail bouncing in excitement. "Really, Tansy. You can't climb through people's windows without permission."

"I climb through *your* window," she pointed out.

"I know, but you've got into enough trouble with Mum today already."

"Trouble?" Dad echoed.

"She's in disgrace at the moment for stealing my mother's sunflower seeds," I explained. "Mum ordered me to teach her to behave."

"Can you teach a squirrel good behaviour?" Jessica glanced over her shoulder and groaned. "Spike, don't tread that into the carpet."

"Hang on." Dad ran through the door to the living room. "Boys, cut it out!"

"They're going through a phase of playing with slime," Jessica told me. "Getting slime out of werewolf fur is no joke."

"Ah." I decided to give that one a miss, and Tansy settled herself on my shoulder as we waited for the coast to be clear.

When I entered the living room, I promptly burst into laughter. Ramsey's hedgehog familiar, Prickles, sat atop the giant Lego throne in the corner of the room, wearing a pink dress and a silver tiara. Ramsey himself glowered at me from the sofa, while I spluttered with helpless giggles.

"Oh my god." I pulled out my camera from my bag. "I need to commit that image to memory forever."

"If you dare to take a picture of me in this state of indignity, I shall put bristles on every seat you sit on for the next year," said Prickles.

"Ooh." Luckily, nobody but my brother and I could

understand the hedgehog's speech. "I'd like to see you try that."

"I think it's very fetching." Tansy sprang from my shoulder onto the sofa, causing my brother to scowl.

Ramsey had dressed down for the weekend, but even in casual clothes, he exuded authority. His blond hair was combed flat—though it looked slightly damp, as though one of the boys had upended a cup of water on his head, which was entirely possible—and his shirt and jeans were pristine. Ramsey and I both looked nothing like our dad, except I'd probably got my height from him, whereas Ramsey towered over me the way Mum did. Coupled with his scowling expression, it was a wonder the boys had had the nerve to kidnap his familiar and stick the unfortunate hedgehog in an embarrassing costume.

Dad settled between me and Ramsey on the sofa and offered a smile. "Tell us the latest news."

I shrugged, conscious of the children in the room. "Not much to tell."

Most of the Head Witch drama I was involved in wasn't remotely suitable for young ears, and neither were certain recent events like dead bodies showing up in the woods and half my family getting possessed by a demon. Admittedly, those events had played a part in Ramsey's decision to reconnect with our dad, who he'd scarcely spoken to since he'd split up from Mum when we were kids. The pair of us had spent several days sprinkling sage along the paths in the forest that circled my dad's cottage so his shifter wife and kids could go for a run in the woods without fearing they'd be jumped by another monster. Nothing like being possessed by a demon to mend old family wounds.

None of that constituted a family-friendly discussion, and since Dad had been witness to most of it anyway, there wasn't any *recent* news to share. Unless he wanted to hear the intricacies of learning how to cast tricky spells using the sceptre, the giant ceremonial wand that I was theoretically supposed to carry with me everywhere but had left at home today. No doubt my mother would be waiting to lecture me on the dangers of leaving the house without the sceptre when I returned, but I drew the line at bringing a volatile magical instrument into a house with small children. Demons or no demons.

I steered the subject over to Dad's job in magical construction instead. I'd much rather hear about wizards' house extension projects gone wrong than discuss the least fun parts of dealing with the coven's council of witches, and between that and watching Tansy's amusing antics, the morning raced by. Before I knew it, the clocks were striking noon, and Ramsey got to his feet.

"I have to go," he announced. "Come on, Prickles."

I stifled a grin as Prickles waddled over to him, shedding his undignified costume in the process. "Where do you have to go on a Saturday? Work, by any chance?"

Ramsey grunted, helping his familiar remove the silver tiara. "Something like that. Don't you have work to be getting on with too?"

"Not on the weekend." I turned to Dad. "I have somewhere I need to be this afternoon as well, but I can stay another hour or so."

"Where, exactly?" Ramsey's attention sharpened. "A date with that Harvey?"

Anyone would think Harvey and I hadn't been romantic partners for going on two months. "Actually, I'm going to the local Sky Hopper match this afternoon. I've volunteered as a photographer."

"You did *what?*" Ramsey asked in tones that would have been more appropriate if I'd said I'd volunteered to become a stripper. "That's not your job."

Since when did he care? "Bit late now, since I already said yes."

Ramsey gave no further argument until we'd said our goodbyes and departed the cottage for home. Then I addressed the manticore in the room. "What's the problem?" I asked. "You *bought* me the camera. Would you rather I used it to take photos of your familiar in silly costumes?"

"Yes," he said tersely. "Why did you feel the need to involve yourself in matters that aren't part of your Head Witch duties?"

I should have figured we were long overdue for an argument. "I thought we established that I'm allowed hobbies."

"Hobbies that involve going to high-profile events?" he said. "You do realise the press will be there, don't you?"

"Not inside the town." I hadn't thought of that, actually, but a Sky Hopper game was a world away from a press conference. "I sent those two reporters packing the last time we spoke, didn't I? We haven't seen them since."

"Yes, you did," he said grudgingly.

"See, it's not hard to admit that I sometimes have good ideas," I added. "Like bringing you to visit Jessica and the kids."

"They put slime in my *hair*."

"Did they?" I'd wondered why his hair had been wet when I'd shown up. "They're kids, Ramsey. You'd be more used to them if you spent more time outside of the office."

"She's right, you know." Tansy jumped onto his shoulder. "You know you'll have to deal with worse if you ever end up having kids, right?"

"What?" He jerked his head away from her fluffy tail. "No. I don't."

"Don't know, or don't want kids?" I queried, more out of surprise than anything else. I didn't think we'd ever discussed the subject since we'd been kids ourselves. Some things were too weird to contemplate, and my brother settling down and having a family of his own was one of them.

"Do *you* want kids?" he retaliated.

"Sure, someday," I replied. "Not my priority at the moment."

"Good" was his reply.

"What's that supposed to mean?" Did he think Harvey and I had been intimate? *I wish.* We barely got time to sneak in a weekly date when I wasn't at work or dealing with other responsibilities, with the added complication that I was stuck living in my old bedroom in my mother's house. Hardly a romantic setting.

Ramsey glanced sideways at me. "Any children we have are likely to be in the running to become the next coven leader."

My heart sank into a familiar plunge. "*I'm* not the next coven leader, Ramsey. There's no reason the title has to stay in our family forever."

His eyes narrowed. "Haven't we talked about this?"

"About *me*, yes, and I said I'm not interested," I said frostily. "And you can keep my hypothetical children out of this too."

"It's not me you have to worry about," he said. "Our family has a reputation far beyond our own circle."

My shoulders stiffened. "Isn't it enough that I'm Head Witch when I never intended to get involved in this crap? Most of the coven wouldn't vote me in as leader if it was between me and Aunt Shannon. Hell, even *Mum* wouldn't vote for me."

"That's untrue," Ramsey said, though his voice didn't hold its usual ring of confidence. "Our mother believes you're perfectly capable of the role, though you aren't currently living up to your potential."

I'd heard *that* one before, from pretty much every single teacher I'd had at the academy. "Maybe my potential doesn't involve presiding over coven meetings, Ramsey."

This was precisely why I'd left town the instant I'd been legally allowed to and had kept a firm distance between myself and the Wildwood Coven throughout my entire adult life, but when I'd accidentally claimed the sceptre, it was as though all the years I'd spent trying to escape had ceased to matter. I hadn't *quite* figured out what I planned to do when I threw off the burden of being Head Witch and fulfilled my mission, but it had never involved staying in Wildwood Heath, and I certainly didn't want to take over leadership of the coven when my mother retired. Unlike the position of Head Witch, coven leadership was subject to a vote, and my brother was lying to himself if he thought anyone in the coven would pick me to steer them into the future.

He was also deluded if he thought for a minute that I'd willingly subject myself to the humiliation.

"You're perfectly capable of fulfilling the role," he persisted. "You've done it for weeks."

"That doesn't mean I *want* to." I reached down to pick up Tansy, who climbed onto my shoulder and wrapped her fluffy tail around the back of my neck. "You got to decide your own future. Why not me? No, don't tell me I'm allowed to choose. You know that isn't true."

He pinched the bridge of his nose. "It's not about you. It's about the coven's own future. Do you really want to throw away a legacy that's been in our family for hundreds of years?"

This guilt trip had officially gone too far. "What legacy? For that matter, why is it acceptable that Grandma managed to make enemies of demons but not that I left town to make something of my own life?"

"You're still set on leaving?" He exhaled in a sigh. "You know, I really thought you'd matured."

"Being mature doesn't mean letting my family members make my decisions for me. Pretty sure it's the opposite, in fact."

Rustling in the treetops warned that my magic was responding to my anger, drawing in any nearby wildlife. I'd never quite mastered the tight control most of my family members had over their abilities, and when emotions ran high, magic pretty much leaked out of my pores. The birds circling overhead didn't do my argument any favours but further underlined why I was utterly unsuited for the role of coven leader.

I wouldn't lie: it was also a relief. When the forest had been infested by monsters from the afterworld, they'd driven away the majority of the local animals, and while that left me with fewer targets to respond to my erratic magic, I'd missed the chirping birds and scampering rodents who'd usually inhabited the forest. I liked the Wildwood. The trees and animals didn't judge me. Unlike some people.

My brother and I walked the rest of the way to the house in silence, our brief truce having thoroughly evaporated. What had he expected me to say, that I'd given up every belief I'd held since I'd been old enough to grasp my family's expectations of my life? The notion of surrendering my freedom was almost intolerable enough for me to act on the escape plans that had lurked in the back of my mind for the past few months—but there was no escape, not as long as I held the sceptre.

*That won't be forever,* I told myself. *Don't think about that. Think about Harvey and the Sky Hopper match.*

My mother waited outside the house, where she greeted me with the ominous words "Robin, I've been looking for you."

"Why?" Oh no. I hadn't told her about my upcoming stint as a photographer, hoping that she'd stick to her word and keep out of what I did with my weekends. Apparently not. "You knew I was going to Dad's."

"The coven's received some sad news," she said. "The leader of the flower club is dead."

"Who… Araminta?" Had she forgotten the flower club's former leader and I hadn't been remotely friendly with one another? "What do you mean, 'the coven'? She's not—she *wasn't*—an active member."

"She was your grandmother's friend and well respected within the coven," Mum said. "It's your job as Head Witch to offer your condolences to everyone affected."

She had to be joking. "I already have a commitment today. How'd she die, anyway?"

It might be a callous question, but Araminta—with her blond wig, caustic temper, and fanatical commitment to the annual flower contest—hadn't seemed the sort to just keel over.

"I don't know the details," she said. "Only that the neighbour found her lying in her back garden among the flowers."

"Sorry to hear that." I wasn't. She'd been downright rude to me and had caused no end of trouble in the recent flower contest, which had ended in someone dead. Araminta hadn't turned out to be the instigator, but she'd shown no qualms about turning her back on the underhanded tactics her fellow flower club members used. I wasn't about to go out of my way to visit the presumably small number of people who *were* sorry at her passing.

I walked past Mum into the house and found Kimberly had left lunch out on the table. One of the perks of living at home was our family's chef, but the delicious bacon sandwich was somewhat overshadowed by my mother's judgemental stare while I was eating. I didn't think Araminta's few mourners would be *that* bothered if I waited until Monday morning to send them a condolence letter, but Mum was adamant. When I went upstairs to fetch my camera, I returned to find her hovering at the foot of the stairs like a statue.

"Look, I have to go." I stepped around her and made for the front door. "I promised I'd take photos at the Sky Hopper match. I did tell you I had plans, didn't I?"

"The Sky Hopper match?" she asked. "Absolutely not. Didn't I tell you to avoid public events?"

"The match is *inside* the town, Mum," I said. "The demon would have a hard time getting past the circle of sage Ramsey put around the forest."

Grandma's demonic enemies might have me on their hit list, but we'd been thorough when we'd placed our protections, and the entire town was circled by an unbroken barrier of sage. A smaller circle encased the part of the forest encompassing Dad's cottage and the road where my mother's house and the coven headquarters were located. The Sky Hopper field might be outside that smaller circle, but it wasn't like I was taking a broomstick ride across the country. The odds of me being attacked by one of Grandma's demonic enemies were incredibly low, but since Mum was one of the people who'd been possessed by the demons in question, her view of the matter was slightly biased.

"Take the sceptre," she ordered.

"That won't make a difference." Demons were effectively ghosts with nastier personalities, and even my sceptre had its limitations when it came to dealing with disembodied monsters. Besides, carrying a giant stick with a glowing purple gem did not help me avoid drawing unnecessary attention.

"All the more reason for you to stay at home."

*I should have expected this.* Everyone had reacted in

different ways to the demons' attack, and Mum was no exception. She hated losing control, and the demon's possession had struck at the heart of her deepest fear, with the result that she'd become even more of a micromanager than she had been previously. My work schedule had been abruptly adjusted to make room for extra magic lessons and focusing on preparation for the next attack, and while I might have rejoiced in having less paperwork to deal with, the constant lectures were starting to wear on me.

Luckily, at that moment, Tansy ran past the window with an entire sunflower head in her mouth.

"That squirrel!" Mum ran for the back door. "If you *must* go, then take the sceptre, Robin. That's an order."

I hid a smile, certain that Tansy had manufactured a distraction on purpose but equally certain that Mum would follow me all the way to the Sky Hopper field if I didn't let her win this part of the argument. I ran back upstairs to grab the sceptre and then left the house before Mum changed her mind.

With the sceptre in one hand and my camera in the other, I followed the forest path, this time bypassing Dad's cottage towards the sound of a cheering crowd. While I'd never been as big a Sky Hopper fan as some, the fact that Harvey was team captain had increased my interest manifold, and the match was a welcome chance to forget both my family's arguments and the demons hunting me down. Who could ask for more?

Before the Sky Hopper match kicked off, I met Harvey and the others at the edge of the grassy pitch, where they'd gathered to talk strategies. The sceptre attracted more attention than I'd have liked, but it was easy enough to ignore the whispers in favour of watching the players. They stood in a bright huddle in their red uniforms as Harvey gave a pre-game pep talk, his shiny captain's badge glowing in the afternoon sun. They'd got lucky with the weather, given how unpredictable late summer in England could be.

Tansy came scurrying over, having returned from tormenting my mother, and clambered onto my shoulder. "Nice to see the team getting along."

"It is," I agreed, thinking of the last time I'd been with the whole group in close quarters. Admittedly, that had been a while ago, and under the slightly worrisome circumstances of the murder of their former captain. Since then, though, Harvey had redoubled his efforts to bring the team together, and it seemed to be paying off.

"They still need a new mascot," Tansy added. "I recommend a red squirrel."

"Tansy, they have red uniforms. They wouldn't be able to see the badge." I still didn't quite understand why they'd picked an extinct bird as their mascot, but the dodo was synonymous with the local team by this point. "Let's say hi."

As I approached, Cole, burly and dark skinned, waved me over with a smile. "Hey, it's Robin. Everyone want to pose for some pre-game photos?"

"Ready when you are." I held my camera up, and the team enthusiastically gathered around.

Harvey got everyone sorted in order so that the taller members like Cole and Gwen didn't block the smaller ones like Everly and Gabriel from view. I was pleased to see Tomas standing next to Gabriel—the two had *not* got along when the latter had first joined the team—while I snapped photos from various angles. Tansy photobombed a few of them, preening and showing off her fluffy tail.

"Yes, you're very cute." I shooed her out of the frame. "Harvey, did you want any more pictures?"

"I think that'll do," he said. "Everyone, go and make your last preparations, okay?"

As the team departed, he strode over and hugged me. "Hey, Robin. Sorry I didn't have time to say a proper hello earlier."

"It's all right. I should have got here sooner." I didn't want to ruin the mood by mentioning my argument with Mum or my clash with my brother, so I added, "I was visiting Dad. When I wasn't stopping Tansy from raiding Mum's sunflowers, that is."

"Oi." Tansy pouted, and I reached out to pick her up before an overenthusiastic Sky Hopper fan trod on her tail.

"Oh, fun," said Harvey. "Was your brother there?"

"Amazingly, yes," I replied. "He even let the boys put slime in his hair and dress up his familiar."

"He did?" He cracked a grin. "I wish I'd seen."

"I didn't get a photo of that, but I *did* get one of Prickles in a dress and tiara." I grinned back, while Tansy let out a loud squeak of laughter.

"That's certainly a mental image, Robin," he said. "You're okay, though? I mean, does your family know you're here?"

He knew me too well. "Yes, but if my mother shows up in the middle of the match, I might need to borrow a spare broomstick."

His brow arched. "Is that likely?"

"I wouldn't have said so, but when I told her I was a volunteer photographer, I might as well have told her I'd signed up to solo pilot a spaceship to Mars."

"Awkward." He glanced behind him as one of the other players shouted his name. "We have to start the game. Will you be all right?"

"Of course. Don't worry, she's not going to show up." I indicated the waving players. "Go to your team. Don't let my ridiculous family put you off your game."

While the teams assembled on the pitch, I climbed to my reserved seat in the prime position in the stands and settled in to watch. Tansy perched on my shoulder, munching a sunflower seed, while I angled my camera to capture the teams assembling on either side of the pitch.

"Your mother's not going to show up," Tansy said in my ear. "She told me herself when she'd stopped berating me over stealing from the garden."

"Good." Though not for the first time, I fervently wished I'd been allowed to leave the sceptre behind. While I propped it between my legs so I could better balance the camera, the purple glow was a constant reminder that I was separated from the laughing, chattering crowd by a barrier that wouldn't go away until I'd fulfilled the sceptre's mission.

And then what? Would my future hold any more Sky Hopper games, or would my family force me into walking away? The thought of a life without Harvey in it repelled me, but it was getting harder and harder to ignore the tightening noose of my family's expectations around my neck. Yet Harvey wasn't the only person I'd lose if I turned my back on Wildwood Heath. My best friend, Piper, my cousin, Rowan—even Chloe, my workaholic assistant. All of them had played a part in the new life I'd forged out of the old, and I couldn't imagine being anywhere other than here.

Even if Tansy did keep getting in front of my camera lens as I snapped pictures of the teams preparing to mount their broomsticks.

"I wish they'd wear bigger badges." She craned her neck. "I can't tell which team is which."

"You just want everyone to wear badges of giant red squirrels regardless of what team they're on."

"Obviously." She flicked her tail impatiently. "Are they going to start the match yet?"

"Yes. Simmer down. Harvey has to greet the other team captain first." My heart fluttered when he caught my eye and smiled at the camera. "Then they'll bring out the hoops."

I didn't *quite* get the intricacies of all the Sky Hopper rules, but the gist was that each team had a certain number of hoops that they needed to pass along a row of players called Falcons while fending off Vultures—members of the other team whose role was to steal the other team's hoops. When one of the team captains claimed the last hoop, the game was won. That made Harvey both essential and also lucky enough to be out of the line of attack, so I wasn't too worried he might suffer any injuries.

At the sound of a whistle from the referee, the broomsticks rose into the sky. I'd adjusted the camera's settings already, so it was just a matter of turning it in the right direction to capture all the action. When Tansy started pouting at my insistence that she keep her furry nose out of the way of the lens, I loaned her my phone so she could play on my Pokémon Go app. That kept her entertained for a while—until she suddenly jumped onto my shoulder, tail ramrod straight and twitching. "I don't believe it."

"What?" I didn't look away from the game. "Did a rare Pokémon get away from you again?"

"No. Look over there." Her tail pointed towards my camera screen, where I spied a red blot amid the crowd in the stands opposite. Through the magnified camera lens, there was no mistaking the source… another red squirrel.

"Huh." I squinted, but with or without the aid of the camera, the other side of the pitch was too far off to determine if the squirrel was accompanied by a person. "You can make a new friend."

"I'm supposed to be the only red squirrel in town!" Tansy squeaked indignantly. "That squirrel is now my arch-nemesis."

"Calm down." I returned my attention to the match, which was somewhat difficult with an angry squirrel bouncing up and down on my shoulder. "If you stop wriggling, I'll be able to check and see if it came alone."

I zoomed in on the seats opposite, and two brooms crashed into one another in midair. As I hastily zoomed out again to see what had caused the collision, Tansy leapt onto the camera and knocked off my aim.

"Tansy!" I grabbed the camera with both hands to keep from dropping it. "What's got into you?"

"There's an alien on the pitch!"

*Okay, she's lost it.* I lowered the camera into my lap and peered out over the grass to see what had her so agitated.

There, I spied a strange dark shape below the pair of broomsticks that had crashed. Not an alien but something large and glistening and jet-black. "Is that… a slug?"

"It's a monster!" Tansy yelped.

"Not quite." I leaned forwards in my seat. "It's massive, but that's definitely a slug."

A slug the size of a person. Was this some kind of practical joke? The two players hadn't seen it coming, and while one of the two riders had managed to grip his broomstick to keep from falling off, the other wasn't so lucky. He tumbled out of the air, and I winced when he landed on the slug with the effect of someone barrelling into a trampoline at speed—except with a lot more slime.

"Poor guy." I could think of several people who'd find it amusing to conjure up a giant slug, but not in the middle of a Sky Hopper game. What was going on?

The other players flew out of formation to look down at the grass, and shouts arose from the crowd as a second slug appeared in front of the stands opposite, drenching the front row in slime. This included the referee, whose microphone made a horrible spluttering noise and went silent. *Uh-oh.*

"Tansy, did you see who did that?" Anyone might have pulled out a wand amongst the spectators, but you'd think someone else in the crowd would have noticed their neighbour conjuring up a giant slug.

"No," Tansy answered. "Your boyfriend's getting back to the game, look."

"Guess he doesn't have much choice." I watched Harvey call his team back into formation, though the other team had considerably more difficulty. The poor guy who'd hit the slug had managed to crawl away, but he was drenched in slime that made it hard for him to remount his broomstick.

Then a scream from the other side of the pitch warned of a third slug's appearance.

"Robin!" yelped Tansy. "You have to do something."

"Do what?" I couldn't reach any of the slugs from up here, and even if I could, there was no way I'd risk using my sceptre on them in case I accidentally hit someone in the crowd. My sceptre didn't really do subtlety. "I can freeze them, but that won't stop whoever's conjuring them." With half the crowd on their feet, picking out one individual was like… well, like spotting a red squirrel amid a sea of crimson uniforms.

"A reversal spell!" Tansy squeaked. "If they were conjured up by magic, it'll make them disappear."

"And if not?" Reversal spells didn't work in all cases, and with the sceptre, the potential for disaster was even higher than usual.

*Think, Robin.* Amazing how I could go through months of Head Witch training and yet everything went flying out of my head as soon as it mattered. Not that giant slugs were a situation I'd prepared for. Someone had to act, though, and the crowd seemed to have collectively decided "panic" was the only option instead. Lifting my head, I locked eyes with Harvey, whose alarmed expression caught at my heart.

*All right, then.* Tucking my camera into my bag, I climbed to my feet and began to edge along the row of seats. At first, people grumbled, then they saw my sceptre and started whispering instead. My pulse thrummed with nerves. *Don't screw this up, Robin,* I thought.

Upon reaching the stairs, I raised the sceptre and pointed it at one of the huge bulbous slugs. With a sweeping motion, I cast a reversal spell, and a bolt of purple light shot from the sceptre's end. The light engulfed the slug, causing everyone nearby to shield their eyes, including me.

When the light cleared, the slug was nowhere to be seen. "Thanks, Tansy," I breathed. "Now for the others."

"It's still there," she squeaked in my ear. "It's just gone back to normal size."

"Has it?" I peered down the stairs. Sure enough, in place of the giant monstrosity, a normal-sized slug lay in a bed of slime and grass. "Well, at least it's much more manageable at that size."

Bolstered, I aimed at the next slug and cast the same reversal spell, causing the slug to shrink to a less terrifying size. I took aim at the third and final slug, and the resulting flash of light brought a wave of cheers from the slime-drenched crowd. My face heated, in a good way for once, especially when the players joined in the chant.

"I told you you could do it," Tansy said smugly. "Hey, that guy's helping out."

Someone in the crowd had conjured up a bucket, and the referee wasted no time in levitating the slugs into it. His microphone evidently hadn't survived, so I couldn't hear what he was saying, but with the pitch slug-free, the match was officially back on.

Not that the crowd was entirely paying attention. As I climbed back to my seat, whispers erupted around me, concerning who'd been responsible for the unwanted visitor, while the number of people trying to grab my arm made it near impossible to get at my camera. I finally reached my seat when cheering broke out, indicating that I'd missed the moment Harvey had caught the last hoop, ending the game.

I joined in with the applause, whispering, "Dammit. I should have stayed on the stairs."

"No, you shouldn't," Tansy replied. "There's someone over there who looks suspiciously like a reporter."

"There isn't, is there?" I didn't have her high vantage point, so I'd have to take her word for it. "They shouldn't have been allowed in."

Amid the cheering, Tansy leaned over to speak into my ear. "I'm going to look around."

"For what?"

"If the prankster is here, they'll probably vanish as soon as people start leaving." She jumped off my shoulder and scurried away.

Hoping she managed to avoid the crush, I returned my attention to the pitch and got a few photos of the teams congratulating one another. Harvey's team might have won, but the knowledge that someone had wanted the match to stop altogether left a bad taste in my mouth.

When the crowd began to make their meandering way towards the exits, I got to my feet too. I'd lost sight of Tansy, but I managed to avoid being grabbed until I reached the stairs again and someone thrust a microphone into my face.

"Head Witch!" cried a familiar voice. "Do tell us how it felt to be the hero of the hour?"

I gaped at the two red-cloaked figures—Clarice and Speck from the *Blue Moon*, the local tabloid, who I'd last seen during an interview that I distinctly remembered telling them would be my last.

"You're not supposed to be here." I nudged the microphone out of the way and sidestepped, trying to use the crowd's momentum to shake them off.

"We came with the other team," said Clarice, slightly apologetically. "We didn't know the match would be *inside* Wildwood Heath when we signed up to cover this story. We've turned over a new leaf, and now, we're focusing on magical sports."

*As opposed to gossiping about my family?* "Good for you. There's no need to talk to me, then, is there?"

"We don't want to interview you about being Head Witch this time," Speck insisted. "You did a fantastic job getting rid of those monstrous creatures."

"I haven't the faintest idea where they came from," I replied. "Can you find someone else willing to talk? Like someone from the actual team, that is?"

"Your boyfriend?"

*Okay, maybe not.* I was about to say as much when Tansy enacted a flying leap and knocked the microphone out of Clarice's hand. While the two reporters dove to retrieve it, I escaped for real this time.

"Thanks, Tansy." I caught her in my hand and placed her on my shoulder. "They always show up when you don't need them. Like an infestation."

We escaped via one of the paths into the forest, where I found a quiet spot to wait for Harvey. While my instincts told me to run far away from those reporters, I wanted to make sure no more slugs made an appearance, and despite what I'd told the press, I *did* want to know where they'd come from in the first place.

"Wish I'd had my camera zoomed in on the crowd," I whispered to Tansy. "Maybe then I'd have been able to see who set those slugs loose."

"It was definitely that squirrel," Tansy insisted.

"I doubt it." I'd lost sight of her fluffy nemesis in the crowd, too, but I drew the line at going back to look for a squirrel. "Only a human can use a wand."

"What if it wasn't a wand?"

We debated back and forth for several minutes as the crowd dispersed. Soon enough, I spied Harvey making his way out of the field with the rest of the team in tow. It was unsurprising that none of them wanted to stay on the pitch and risk another giant slug materialising on top of them, but they'd also brought an unwanted entourage in the form of a certain pair of reporters.

Oblivious to his unwanted stalkers, Harvey approached me. "Hey, Robin. Good thinking there."

"Thanks." I tensed, hearing the snap of a camera that wasn't mine. "Just so you know, there's a certain pair of reporters looking for people to hassle, and you're top of their list."

"Those two from the *Blue Moon*?" He grimaced. "I thought you sent them packing."

"They claim they're covering sports now, and they got through a loophole by claiming they didn't know the match was in Wildwood Heath."

Harvey swore. "All right. You should go, Robin, before they ambush you again."

"You too, but I wanted to ask if you saw where those slugs came from. Are they still on the pitch?"

"The other team captain said he sent them to the coven to be checked over. As for where they came from, your guess is as good as mine."

I groaned. "They sent them to my mother. Didn't they know I was in the audience?"

Not that I'd wanted to carry a bucket of slugs around, but I didn't like to think of how Mum would react to them showing up on the doorstep right after I'd confidently informed her that the match would be a trouble-free zone.

"You're off duty, so I guess he didn't want to bother you." He glanced over his shoulder. "Oh no. Cole's talking to the reporters."

"Dammit." At another flash of the camera, I retreated farther down the path. "All right, I'm off. See you soon?"

"Of course." He hugged me and then ran to rescue his teammates from the reporters. Hoping he managed to escape an interrogation, I ducked into the forest.

I was less than inclined to think Clarice and Speck had had a change of heart and decided to give up their trouble-making ways, but just sharing photos of the match would be enough to irk my family members. Typically, Mum was waiting outside the house when I approached, and from her thunderous expression, she'd already found the bucket of slugs.

"Mum." I forced a smile. "Anything you need my help with?"

"Don't play games with me," she snapped. "You know perfectly well that someone has decided to leave a threatening message for the coven."

"You mean the bucket of slugs?" They might be annoying, but they hardly constituted a threat to the coven. "Someone conjured up giant slugs on the pitch at the Sky Hopper game as a practical joke, yes, but I shrank them to normal size without any issues."

Tansy popped up. "You can put them in Aunt Shannon's office."

"Don't be absurd." Mum's lips compressed. "I knew it was a bad idea for you to go to that match."

"This would have happened if I hadn't been there too," I pointed out. "I wasn't the target."

"How do you know that?" Ramsey appeared behind Mum in the hallway. "You might have been."

"Yes, because my enemies are known for summoning giant slugs before they bring out the demons." I gave an eyeroll. "It was a prank, and a fairly harmless one at that."

"We'll see." Mum swept away from the house, presumably to deal with the aforementioned bucket of slugs, while Ramsey remained planted in front of the door.

"What?" I took a step closer to him. "If I'd stayed at home, there'd have been an even bigger fuss. Nobody else was going to get rid of the slugs."

"You used the sceptre for that?"

"Yes, why?" I walked around him through the open front door. "I thought Mum *wanted* me to use the sceptre more often. I really can't do anything right, can I?"

Irked, I walked through the living room and kitchen to the back garden, where my best friend, Piper, was tending to Mum's flowerbeds. She offered me a smile. "Hey, Robin. How'd the match go? I saw a bit of it from here but not who won."

"Harvey's team won, but we had a small disruption in the form of a bunch of giant slugs." I sat down on the carved bench next to the bird feeder. "That's what Mum's dealing with, so expect her to be in a foul mood when she comes back."

Piper cracked up laughing. "Oh, that's a good one. Giant slugs?"

I cast a glance over Mum's pristine flowerbeds, glad the other team captain hadn't sent them here instead. "I don't know who was responsible, but Mum thinks it's my mortal enemies sending a threatening message to the coven."

Piper's brow wrinkled. "Seems more like someone thought the match lacked excitement."

"Or some *squirrel*." Tansy scaled the bird feeder on swift feet.

"You know squirrels can't cast spells."

"Doesn't mean they can't plot and scheme," Tansy retaliated. "I don't trust that red squirrel. None of them are trustworthy except me.

Piper gave me a curious look, having only heard my side of our brief exchange. "Squirrels?"

"Tansy saw another red squirrel and decided it's her archnemesis," I explained.

Piper snorted. "Sounds about right. I wonder who it belonged to, though. There aren't too many other red squirrels around."

"Might not be local." The squirrel was more likely than not to be a witch's familiar, which wasn't suspicious on its own, but who knew, maybe Tansy's suspicions weren't unwarranted.

Regardless of who was responsible, why on earth would someone set a bunch of slugs loose at a Sky Hopper game? What had they hoped to achieve?

3

The following day, I came downstairs to find my mother at the kitchen table, sipping black coffee. Her cat familiar, Horace, lay on the sofa alongside Grandma's familiar, Carmilla. Both of them hissed at me when I tried to stroke them, which was kind of unfair but what I'd come to expect from the house's other animals.

I grabbed breakfast and watched Tansy act like her usual chaotic self in the garden, jumping at the bird feeder and generally asserting her dominance over the territory. No signs of the other red squirrel had shown up, as far as I knew, but Mum wore an expression that suggested a dozen rodents had shredded her favourite slippers in the night.

"Where's Ramsey?" I asked in an attempt to break the silence.

"No idea," she said frostily. "At work, I assume."

Nothing new there. My brother would probably have slept at the office if he could have got away with it; in fact, he'd have preferred not to bother with mundane inconveniences like sleep at all. If ever there was a chance to sign up to become a cyborg, Ramsey would be first in line.

"All right." I pushed my plate away and stood up. "I'm going to see Rowan, and then—"

"No, you aren't," she said.

"Excuse me?" I tensed. "Sunday is my day off."

"You took yesterday off."

"Yes, and I got in plenty of practise with my sceptre when I was getting rid of those giant slugs." Was one Sky Hopper game justification enough for her to monopolise the one day on which I had no responsibilities? "Besides, Rowan's flat is perfectly safe."

"It's not a safety issue," Mum said in calmer tones. "I wanted to check that there haven't been any more incidents like the one at the match yesterday."

"What, giant slugs?" I bit back a laugh. "Didn't you get rid of them?"

"This is no laughing matter," she said. "The slugs were summoned using a powerful curse."

"Compared to the demons, giant slugs are hardly a terrifying threat," I replied. "I guarantee if there was a demon around, they'd have attacked me, not the flowerbeds."

"The curse was powerful enough that no spell I tried was able to undo it."

"Wait… you couldn't?" That was an unusual admission on her part. "Do you want me to try with the sceptre?"

"You can," she said, "but I doubt it'd have any effect. When cast right, curses can only be undone by the person who cast them."

Well, crap. "We don't know who that is."

"Did you see anyone at the match acting suspiciously?"

"No, but there were too many people to focus on a single one." A flash of red drew my gaze to the window, where Tansy leapt after a fleeing pigeon. "Tansy saw another red squirrel and blamed it for everything, but you know she thinks any other red squirrel in the vicinity is her mortal enemy."

"They're rare." She pursed her lips. "Might be worth looking into."

"Oh, come on." This time, I couldn't stop myself from laughing. "Good luck finding a lone squirrel in the Wildwood. There were over a hundred people at the match. Isn't it more likely that one of them cursed the pitch, not a rodent who can't carry a wand?"

"We had everyone vetted before entering," she said. "They passed through the sage barrier. Whoever did this acted against us intentionally, knowing we'd find out."

"That also means nobody was possessed by a demon." If you asked me, that was more important. "Unless you want my numerous enemies to think I'm afraid of my own shadow, I'm not going to flip out over a practical joke. I don't need to make a public statement."

"It sounds like you already did." Mum whipped out a copy of the *Blue Moon*, where my face was plastered all over the front page. *They just had to, didn't they?*

"Clarice and Speck waved a microphone in my face and followed me all the way out of the stands," I told her. "I didn't say anything except that I hadn't a clue where the slugs had come from."

"I thought you knew that any piece of information you give them can be used against you."

"They're claiming to be sports reporters now," I said ineffectually. "Also, since I *stopped* the slugs, they didn't have anything to use against me this time. Trust me."

Mum cast the paper aside. "You wouldn't have had to make a statement if you hadn't been present."

"Yes, I would have, because I'm Head Witch," I pointed out. "Didn't they deliver the slugs to the coven headquarters? Where are they now, sitting in a bucket in a spare room?"

"Something like that." She took in a breath. "When it comes to curses, the intent is never benign, and there's always a chance you were the target."

She just wouldn't let it go. "What does this have to do with me not hanging out with Rowan today? What do you want me to do, call the press?"

"Definitely not," she replied. "No, I've volunteered both of us to clean Araminta's house."

*What?* "Doesn't she have any family to help out?"

"Not local," she said. "If you won't offer any condolences until tomorrow morning, you can at least make things easier for her loved ones."

"There's no reason I can't go and see Rowan afterwards, is there?" I attempted a placating tone. "There's less likely to be killer slugs inside the café than in Araminta's house, you know that."

Mum pursed her lips. "If you must."

With one small victory won, I went into the garden to tell Tansy where I was going. My familiar claimed she was happy to stay at home; it didn't escape my attention that she'd been stashing more sunflower seeds behind a flowerpot. Mum must have been distracted if she'd stopped noticing Tansy's mischief.

The street where the flower club leader had lived was lined with cosy bungalows with bright flowers blooming in the gardens. Araminta's rhododendron-painted door opened at a flick from Mum's wand, and the first thing I noticed was that the inside of the house was oddly bare. Or maybe it seemed that way because the last time I'd been here, she'd moved half the flowers in the garden into the house to stop them from being poisoned by potential saboteurs prior to the flower contest. Sure enough, I peered out the back window and was greeted with a wall of eye-wateringly bright-coloured magical flowers.

"Garden's flourishing, then," I remarked. "I don't think there are any giant slugs out there, somehow."

"No." Mum lifted her head when someone knocked on the front door. "Who's that?"

I swivelled to the front. "Was she expecting visitors?"

Mum walked to the door, and I followed, more out of curiosity than anything else. We were greeted by a grey-haired woman with daisies braided into her curly hair and an unconvincing expression of grief.

"Oh, Lady Wildwood. I'm *so* glad someone volunteered to help clean up Araminta's house—it's been such an awful shock." Crystal's gushing tone was about as convincing as Tansy's denial of stealing Mum's sunflower seeds. The two had been friends, or as close as possible for two scheming competitors in the flower contest, but I didn't trust the woman an inch after her attempts to cheat in the flower contest had unintentionally got someone poisoned to death with thorn-killer toxin. *What does she want?*

"We don't need any assistance here," said Mum in frosty tones, clearly thinking the same. "Did you want anything in particular?"

"Only to express my condolences," said Crystal with maximum insincerity. "And to offer my help if you need it."

"We don't." Mum's flat tone made me stifle an unexpected laugh. She wasn't usually so openly hostile, but without any witnesses except for me, she was free to express her distaste towards Araminta's supposed friend.

Crystal took a step back, her mouth parting. "In that case, I shall leave."

She did so, giving a flounce of her daisy-filled hair, and Mum closed the door with a snap.

I raised a brow. "Bit harsh. Not that she didn't deserve it."

Mum jerked her head towards the door. "That one is trouble."

"What makes you say that?" I didn't disagree, but her reaction seemed a tad extreme. "She doesn't have any reason to poison anyone's plants now the flower contest is over. Unless you thought she might want to steal something?"

"She might," she said. "Anyone who buys illegal poison from the Wizarding Web is not someone who I'd want in my house after I died."

"True enough." It wasn't like Mum to be so blunt, though. She usually covered her emotions in a veneer of politeness, but her odd recent behaviour made her less predictable. "I wonder if she expects to take over as flower club leader. Crystal, I mean. I wouldn't have thought she'd be very popular with the others after the thorn-killer-toxin incident."

Granted, the whole club was made up of backstabbing retired witches who quite literally had nothing better to do with their time than poison one another's flowers and generally make a nuisance of themselves.

A thought tickled at the back of my mind. *Thorn-killer toxin...*

When Mum didn't reply, I glanced sideways at her. "You don't think Araminta died of unnatural causes, do you?"

Crystal had had no scruples about dousing Ami's flowers with thorn-killer toxin, but did that extend to poisoning an actual person? Crystal and Araminta hadn't exactly been on good terms the last I'd seen, but the same could be said of the entire flower club.

Mum drew in a breath. "It's pure conjecture at this stage, but Araminta was in perfect health before she died."

"Meaning something *might* be amiss." Why hadn't I thought of it earlier? Perhaps Mum's paranoia wasn't entirely out of left field after all.

She eyed me. "Now do you see why we need to be here?"

"Not really." If Araminta had been poisoned by one of her fellow flower-growing witches, there was little either of us could do to mitigate the situation. "I'm unlikely to have been the target. Just like the slugs."

Mum pushed open the back door onto the maze of bright flowers. I followed, sneezing at the potent smell of pollen. "So you didn't actually want to clean up the house? What are you looking for out here?"

"This is where Araminta's body was found," she said over her shoulder, pulling out her wand. "By a neighbour."

She proceeded to cast several spells—detection charms, at a guess—while I craned my neck, trying to see over the neighbour's fence and the thick hedge bordering the garden. No luck. The hedge was dense enough that I wouldn't have known if someone was staring straight back at me from the other side.

When she'd finished casting spells, Mum lowered her wand. "No magical interference, but that doesn't rule out an internal cause of death."

"What, poison?" Tricky to prove; half the plants here might be poisonous for all I knew. "I'm pretty sure the police are the ones who are meant to investigate possible murders. I mean, haven't they looked at her body?"

"They will." She cast a glance around the garden. "However, until they verify the cause of death, it's worth seeing if she left any clues behind."

"Clues as to her own murder?" Baffled, I watched her walk between rows of towering plants. "Then why bring *me* here? I thought you didn't like me doing detective work without permission from the police. What changed your mind?"

"Araminta said…" She paused for a moment then plunged ahead. "According to my mother, she claimed that she intended to have revenge on her mortal enemies when she died."

"Grandma told you that?" Revenge on her mortal

enemies? That did sound like Araminta, but it was uncharacteristic of my mother to follow Grandma's lead. As a ghost, the former Head Witch was far more eccentric than she'd been as a living person and was a royal nuisance to boot.

Mum waved her wand again, and then she shook her head. "No, the only spells or curses I can find here are ones intended to make her plants grow."

"Curses." The word pinged inside my head. "You don't think *she* was responsible for the slugs… do you?"

Curses couldn't be cast by dead people, right? Yet Mum wore an expression that was entirely serious. "It's possible."

I snorted. "Did she claim that she'd unleash revenge by giant slugs?"

"She didn't specify, but a curse intended to wreak havoc on plants and flowers sounds very much like Araminta's work."

"What's that got to do with Sky Hopper, though?" I asked. "The field is way out in the forest."

"It's also where the flower contest took place."

Oh. That made a little more sense, but it didn't stop her from being *dead*. "Dead people can't use magic. Even Grandma knows that."

"Curses are tricky." Mum lowered her voice and retraced her steps to the house. "They can be cast on people or on objects… even places."

"I know that," I said, "but the curse is nullified when the person responsible dies, isn't it?"

"There are exceptions, and Araminta explicitly said she intended to have revenge *after* her death."

"She might have been posturing." Though I couldn't deny that unleashing giant slugs on people wouldn't be unlike Araminta, another flower club member was equally likely to have come up with the idea. Especially if one of them had also bumped her off. "Might it have been Crystal who did it?

Maybe she came here to see if her slugs attacked Araminta's garden too."

"The thought crossed my mind," she said, "but if she was the one who murdered Araminta, it wouldn't be wise to draw attention to herself."

"So we potentially have two different criminals." Wonderful. "One of whom might be dead. What's the priority, then? Finding the killer or stopping the curse?"

"Depending on how sophisticated the curse is, it might be that finding Araminta's killer will be enough to bring the curse to an end."

"Araminta's death doesn't need to have been murder for her to unleash a curse on everyone, does it, though?" I queried. "She might have set the curse up to start after her death regardless of the circumstances."

"That is true," she said. "However, I think it's best to start with the assumption that her death was no accident."

How the tables had turned. I was usually the one whose suspicion over deaths from apparent natural causes led me to face denial at every turn, and to hear this kind of speculation from my mother was bizarre to say the least. Especially as she'd dragged *me* into this.

"What do you want, a list of people she interacted with before she died?" I asked. "Because that's more Ramsey's area than ours."

"It shouldn't be too hard to compile a list, considering she rarely left her house except to go into the garden."

"I guess." Pretty much everyone who lived in this part of town was retired and constantly in one another's business, which meant everyone would need to have a solid non–work-related alibi for the time of her death. Tricky.

Someone rang the doorbell, and Mum glanced over that way. "Let's see who it is this time."

4

—————

When Mum opened the door, we found a considerably friendlier face on the other side than the previous visitor. Ami, a curvy witch with short grey hair, gave me a smile. "Oh, hello. I heard the Head Witch was here."

"Ah—hi, Ami." As possibly the only nice member of the flower club, she certainly wasn't someone I'd have expected to visit Araminta, whether she was alive or otherwise.

"You heard?" Mum echoed. "Who told you, exactly?"

"Crystal did," Ami replied promptly. "She was knocking on all our doors, asking if we'd heard the news."

I was surprised that she'd visited Ami, given that Crystal had been responsible for poisoning Ami's flowers and had inadvertently caused her to end up being rewarded a consolation prize in the flower contest instead of being disqualified. "Why would Crystal care that the Head Witch is here?"

"She's a notorious gossip." Ami dropped her voice. "And… I think she's wondering if… if there was anything *untoward* about Araminta's death."

I tensed, not knowing how much Mum wanted me to

35

share. While I was more inclined to trust Ami than I was Crystal, if Araminta *had* been murdered, Ami was theoretically one of the suspects. "We... don't know."

"Oh, don't feel obliged to share with me," Ami added. "I know it's probably in poor taste to ask these questions, though that wouldn't have stopped Araminta from doing the same in similar circumstances, I don't doubt."

"True." I threw caution to the wind. "I heard talk of Araminta making claims that she intended to unleash some kind of curse upon her enemies when she died. Did she say anything like that at flower club meetings?"

Mum gave a frown, but Ami gave a wince. "Yes, she did. Frequently."

"Did she give specifics?" If Araminta had loudly proclaimed her intentions for the whole world to hear, it'd be a lot easier to prove she was responsible.

Mum, who evidently thought otherwise, changed tack. "What Robin means to ask is if you've experienced anything odd in your garden in the past day."

"Funny you should say that," said Ami. "I found my flowers in a terrible state this morning. I wondered if someone had been sabotaging me again, though I couldn't think why they would when there are no other flower contests until *next* summer."

"Did they use thorn-killer toxin?" I asked.

"No... to be truthful, it looked like some kind of animal got at my flowers," she said. "It wasn't poison. Something *ate* them."

"Like giant slugs?"

Surprise flickered across her features. "I wouldn't call them *giant*, but I did certainly see a fair number of slugs in my garden."

"They showed up during the Sky Hopper match yesterday," I explained. "Giant slugs all over the pitch. I had to use my sceptre to shrink them, but they've proven... resilient." I silently congratulated myself for finding a Mum-approved alternative to "the coven leader couldn't get rid of them."

Mum herself cleared her throat. "We believe they're the result of a curse."

"A curse... You mean Araminta's?" A mixture of amusement and horror crossed Ami's face. "I didn't think of that, but I was certainly ranked highly on her list of enemies, I expect."

"She had a list?" I asked.

"A detailed one, according to her rants at flower club meetings," she said. "She used to change the order depending on who'd annoyed her recently, and I expect that I gained a higher position on the list after the incident at the contest over the summer."

"Those meetings sound like a barrel of laughs," I remarked.

Mum pursed her lips, but Ami didn't take offence. "Oh, they used to be fun, before some of the long-term members left and Araminta took over leadership... but I digress. I can't think of any current feuds that would have led to anyone harming her."

"You don't think she was murdered by someone in the club?" I queried. "Who else might have done it?"

"Oh, she had feuds with far more people than the flower club members. Her neighbour, for instance." She indicated the wall on the right-hand side. "She doesn't like most of her family either."

"No shortage of people who might have had reason to bump her off." And plenty of potential targets for giant slug infestations, too. "When did you last see her in person?"

"Hmm... a week ago?" she said. "I haven't been going to flower club meetings since the contest over the summer, but I ran into her at the corner shop, and she seemed fine then."

"Thank you for letting us know," Mum said. "Do you want us to help get rid of those slugs?"

"Would you?" Ami smiled. "I don't want to impose on you, but it'd be most welcome."

"It's no problem." I was all too happy to get out of Araminta's house, and I'd rather help someone with good intentions than try to solve the supposed murder of a witch who hadn't been a nice person at all. "There's nothing else we need to do here, right, Mum?"

She gave the living room a last scan. "No, not at the moment."

Ami beamed. "Thank you, Lady Wildwood."

We left Araminta's house and walked the short distance to Ami's cottage on the adjacent street. She led us through her house to the back garden, where it became immediately obvious where the problem lay. The flowers were a wreck of holes and tattered leaves, courtesy of the considerable number of slugs crawling all over the garden. At least the slugs were normal-sized, not giant monstrosities like on the Sky Hopper pitch, but the sheer number of them indicated someone had been up to no good.

Mum pulled out her wand and waved it in a complex motion, and a shimmering light flashed. I didn't know which spell she'd cast, but when I blinked the dazzle from my eyes, the slugs hadn't so much as budged.

"I thought so," Mum said. "They're not living creatures. They're magically created, the same as the others."

Oh boy. "What do you want to do with them?"

"I can transport them elsewhere, but that's a temporary measure." She shook her head. "Until we resolve the curse, however, it's our only option."

"Send them where?" I was kind of tempted to drop them in Aunt Shannon's garden, though for all we knew, she was already on Araminta's list of enemies.

"I'll send them to the coven headquarters." She waved her wand, and a few slugs disappeared. "I set up several buckets in case there was another incident, as I suspected there would be."

"Troublesome." Ami watched with her mouth turned down at the corners as Mum sent the slugs packing, one slimy group at a time. "You don't think they're in anyone else's gardens, do you?"

"If not now, they will be, if this curse is as widespread as I suspect," said Mum. "Can you do me a favour and ask around?"

"I will." Ami lifted her chin. "I'm not on friendly terms with certain members of the flower club, but if those slugs get into Crystal's garden next, she'll make it everyone's problem."

"I bet." Then a more obvious issue occurred to me. "Wait, are *we* on her list?"

"Almost certainly." Mum spoke in steely tones. "They won't get into *my* garden. It's been warded ever since the flower contest."

*I hope she's right.*

With the last slug banished, Mum and I left the garden and bade farewell to Ami. As we walked away from her house, Mum glanced sideways at me. "I wonder if her neighbours have been affected."

"Whose, Araminta's?" Okay, it was time to nip this one in the bud. "We can't de-slug every garden in town. You'll have people queuing up outside the house, assuming the Head Witch is now offering gardening services."

"That's not why I made the suggestion," Mum said. "If one of her neighbours had a role in her death…"

"Oh no." I raised my hands. "Getting rid of slugs is one thing, but questioning potential murder suspects is the police's business. I thought you didn't want me treading on their toes."

"That was before."

*Before the demons,* I read between the lines. "Mum, I'm not the killer's target. I might end up with giant slugs in my bed, but that's not…" I cut myself off. I'd been going to say, "that's not worth calling the police over," but if *that* happened, I'd hunt down Araminta's murderer myself.

Mum tutted. "Whoever killed Araminta might not have known the level of chaos she'd unleash upon her death, but until we find them, the coven will remain distracted at a time when we cannot afford to be."

"Not everyone." I doubted the other coven members had even noticed anything was awry. "Why not volunteer someone else to take charge of cleaning up the slugs?" Aunt Shannon, for instance. The mental image was amusing if nothing else.

"No," Mum answered. "The more people who realise we're unable to lift the curse ourselves, the more vulnerable we become."

"Then can't you ask Ramsey to talk to Araminta's neighbours?" I asked. "It *is* his job to investigate potential murders. It's not mine, and if her death has nothing to do with any of the people who want *me* dead, getting involved will only put me in the path of another potential killer."

She was silent for a long moment. "Fine."

I'd won this round, but I didn't feel any sense of triumph. Between Mum's paranoia and the knowledge that Araminta had been more vindictive than I'd ever have guessed, tomorrow was already shaping up to be a gruelling day at the office.

Of course, we were making a leap by assuming Araminta was behind the slugs at all. We might be looking in the wrong place. Araminta had been as old as Grandma, and it wasn't that out there to assume her death had been due to natural causes and not murder.

Either way, who on earth had sent the slugs, and what did they want to achieve?

———

I'd been concerned that Grandma would react to the news of Araminta's death by throwing one of her infamous tantrums, but she didn't show up in my office the following morning at all. Neither did Chloe, my assistant, who my mother had borrowed for some reason or other.

Mum had still been acting decidedly *off* when we'd got back from Araminta's house, though she'd agreed to let me spend the rest of the day hanging out with Rowan, with the result that I didn't quite know what to expect from her today. My main task was to write letters of condolence to everyone Araminta had known, which seemed a colossal waste of time given that half of them had probably celebrated when they'd heard the news.

Midmorning, Grandma finally announced herself by appearing on top of my desk and making me jump and smudge my signature on the page. "What are you working on?" She peered over my shoulder. "Condolence letters?"

"Yes." I grabbed my wand to clean up the smudged paper. "Er, did Mum tell you…?"

"Yes, she did tell me Araminta is dead," she said. "Good, she can come to keep me company over here in the afterworld."

I blinked in surprise. "You already have company."

I'd also thought she existed in constant denial about living in the afterworld at all, if you applied the term "living" loosely, but this reaction was infinitely better than her throwing a temper tantrum.

"I don't have any friends over here," she said sadly. "You'll help me get in touch with her when she passes on, won't you?"

"Grandma, I'm not supposed to mess with the afterworld." Given the number of monsters in there that wanted to kill both of us—or worse—she ought to understand that, surely.

Grandma tutted. "Now, it's going to be a bit difficult for you to get rid of the demons with that attitude, isn't it?"

"Don't let Mum hear you say that," I warned. "She doesn't want me putting my life at risk."

Grandma gave a cackle. "A little late for that, isn't it?"

She wasn't wrong, but her attitude wasn't making me any keener on the idea of calling Araminta back from beyond the grave. Did she not care that her old friend was dead, or had she simply been dead herself for long enough not to notice the difference? It also probably wasn't wise for me to point out that she was an unusually strong ghost due to having been a coven leader and Head Witch while she was alive, and it was possible that her friend would simply pass straight into the next stage of the afterlife without sticking around.

Not that I wanted to push Grandma into a rage by giving her an outright refusal and causing her to trash my office again. "Yes, but she likes to pretend this is all within my power to solve if I just take on extra paperwork."

"That she does." She gave another laugh. "Pity she didn't get some sense knocked into her by being possessed."

"Really, Grandma." This callousness was a bit much even for her. "What's the matter with you today?"

"I thought you had more of a sense of humour, Robin." She swept past my desk, knocking over a stack of condolence letters in the process. "I also thought you had more sense than to send letters to people who Araminta would happily have buried in her flowerbeds."

My shoulders tensed. "Do you know about her list of enemies?"

"Obviously."

"Then…" I picked up the papers she'd knocked over. "Then you know that there are a lot of people she promised revenge on after she died too. Was she serious, do you know?"

"Is the sky blue?"

"Meaning yes?" I peered at her smirking, ghostly face. "If she used some kind of curse against anyone who she thinks has wronged her from beyond the grave, we'll have to stop her."

"Certainly not." She scoffed. "The coven could use the excitement."

Reading between the lines, she didn't know of the slug incidents yet, but this was a prime example of why I didn't trust her judgement. As a ghost, she was freed from the restrictions of being Head Witch and coven leader, but her once-sharp mind had grown mercurial and chaotic. She had no ability to get rid of any curse Araminta might have used, being dead, though she knew the wily old flower club leader better than I had.

Mum entered the office, Chloe on her heels. "Have you finished the letters, Robin?"

"Almost." I moved a stack of papers aside and pinned them down with a stapler so that the breeze Grandma conjured up when she drifted past didn't knock them off the desk. "What've you two been doing?"

"Making arrangements" was Mum's enigmatic reply.

"For what?"

"The coven meeting in less than an hour."

I stifled a groan. "What's on the agenda this time?"

"What do you think?"

"Not the slugs?" Though if the buckets had been stored at

the coven's headquarters for the time being, it was only a matter of time before someone started asking questions. "What am I supposed to say, that a dead woman cursed all her supposed enemies to be plagued with magically created slugs that can't be destroyed?"

"Not in so many words," she said. "I'll give the report. Leave it to me."

"All right."

I hastened to finish the condolence letters before handing them over to Chloe to put into the right envelopes. Then I got ready for another joyless meeting with the coven's least interesting members.

The rest of the council and I had a contentious relation-ship at the best of times. Most of them spent meetings arguing for the sake of arguing, while Aunt Shannon did her best to undermine me *and* Mum at any opportunity with the help of my cousin Vanessa. One council member spent all her time knitting, while another only showed up every other Monday. And then there was Mum, whose no-nonsense atti-tude was the only reason anything got done.

As Mum had suggested, I opened the meeting as Head Witch and let her take over from there. In no time at all, the rest of the council had dissolved into an argument over which room to put the buckets of slugs in, and I zoned out, content to let them argue until they ran out of steam.

At least until Aunt Shannon addressed me directly. "The Head Witch understands, I'm sure."

*Understands what?* I fixed on a smile. "Yes?"

Aunt Shannon raised a brow, predictably having guessed that I hadn't been paying attention for the past ten minutes. "I was simply remarking on recent events."

That might mean anything from the demons to the slug infestation. If she'd told the entire council of Grandma's enmity with demons, I'd have expected more of a ruckus, so I'd bet on the latter, but she couldn't know about our suspicions around Araminta's death, surely.

"I understand that we have limited resources as a coven," I said carefully, "and that we should choose what to involve ourselves in wisely."

"Why, of course," she said, "though I wonder if someone was counting on us being willing to overlook a few slugs. Don't forget our image is at stake. That interview you did, for instance…"

"I didn't do an interview." What I'd said to Clarice and Speck barely counted as a statement, but my aunt's senses were as attuned to gossip as Tansy's were to sunflower seeds. "I told the press that I didn't know who was responsible, which is true. If anyone here has any other ideas, do enlighten us."

"A harmless prankster, no doubt," said one of the other witches.

The witch buried in knitting cleared her throat. "Prankster or not, they've targeted the coven. That means it's worth our while to take notice."

"We've noticed." At a warning look from Mum, I added, "There's not much we can do until we know more except speculate unproductively."

Not that these meetings were a shining example of productivity. I was pretty sure nobody had said anything useful in the hour we'd been here, and another hour of arguing followed Aunt Shannon's interruption.

After the meeting finally dragged to an end, Mum waylaid me on the way out the door. "Really, Robin. The slug situation might not be urgent, but it *isn't* insignificant."

"Compared to demons, it is." I crossed the lobby to my office and followed Chloe inside. "Look—what am I expected to do? Did you want me to tell the council that you think

Araminta was murdered and cursed everyone? None of us have proof."

"Yet." She stepped into the office behind me. "And that will change when they finish examining the body."

Right, I'd forgotten about that. "That won't necessarily tie the curse back to her, though. It's not like she wrote down a list of enemies she planned to unleash slugs on."

"That we know of."

I sighed inwardly. "Grandma says Araminta's ghost will show up eventually. If she does, she can speak for herself."

Grandma herself was notably absent, but Mum nodded at my words. "Yes, that's true."

"Of course, the last time the council had to take the word of a ghost, it didn't work out particularly well," I added.

"Speaking of which," she said. "I called the local Reaper's office earlier to set up a meeting. He wasn't in, but I left him a message."

My heart skipped a beat. "You did?"

Did Reapers have offices? The only one I'd met had been Maura, a self-proclaimed retired half-Reaper who wasn't privy to the inner workings of the individuals who reaped the souls of the dead. She knew more than most people did, of course, and my brief glimpse of their world had left me anticipating my next encounter with a Reaper with a mixture of dread and resignation. After all, Reapers were the only ones who stood a chance of helping me solve my demon dilemma, and speaking to the local one would undeniably be far more useful than cleaning up magically conjured slugs. On the other hand, setting up a meeting would seem to indicate that I *was* ready to face the demons… which I wasn't. I might never be.

"As soon as I receive a reply, we'll see if we can discuss our situation," Mum added. "I'm sure he'll be willing to help, as he did before."

*That wasn't permanent, though.* He'd helped Grandma banish the demons for two decades or more, which wasn't insignificant, but they'd broken free at the first opportunity and sworn revenge on her replacement. Aka, me. "Let's hope so. It took long enough to even *find* him."

Reapers didn't show up in the phone book. Probably so people didn't show up on their doorsteps, pleading for their dead loved ones to be returned to the land of the living. I hadn't asked Grandma how she'd gone about contacting the same Reaper twenty-odd years ago, but knowing her, she'd made the demons everyone's problem until he'd shown himself out of sheer exasperation.

Regardless, I had to admit I'd rather meet with a Reaper than spend another hour in a council meeting, discussing the pros and cons of storing buckets of slugs in the building.

5

When lunchtime finally dragged around, I walked to the local café, Were's My Coffee?, to grab a latte and a sandwich. My cousin Rowan was always happy to see me, even when she was on shift behind the counter, and I relished the chance to catch up with her and forget the tribulations of dealing with the council and my grandmother.

The universe had other ideas. No sooner had I placed my order than Ramsey walked in wearing an accusing stare that suggested he intended to arrest the staff for substandard lattes or something.

"Robin." He halted next to me at the counter. "I thought I'd find you here."

"Nice to see you too." I took my order and smiled at Rowan, who eyed Ramsey warily. She'd never quite got over the fact that he'd had her locked in a cell on suspicion of murder, though she was hardly alone in that dubious honour. "Did you want to buy something?"

"No. I'd like to talk to you alone, Robin."

*Oh boy.* "All right."

I took my latte and sandwich outside, wondering if Mum had told him of her suspicions regarding Araminta's death. I *hoped* she had, because it was Ramsey's job to investigate murders, not mine, and I'd been more than ready to wash my hands of the matter and focus on my upcoming meeting with the local Reaper instead.

"What—Ramsey?" I hurried to keep pace with him as he veered over to the police station. "Hang on. I'd like to know what this is all about."

"I thought you knew," he said. "There's been a new development."

"With Araminta?" I followed him through the automatic doors and was immediately set upon by the receptionist, Julian.

"Stop right there," Julian ordered.

"What?" I jerked back, nearly spilling my latte. "Ramsey dragged me in here."

My brother did not come to my rescue. Instead, he inclined his head. "Go on, Julian."

"You can come in when you answer a couple of questions," Julian told me. "What are the names and titles of every member of the council of the Wildwood Coven?"

"I'm sorry, what?"

"It's a security question."

"You have everyone answering security questions?" He had to be joking. "I didn't know I needed to bring notes."

"It's the only way to ensure people are who they say they are."

"You think the demons couldn't just pull that information out of my head?" I looked to Ramsey, but he shook his head at me.

"Answer the question," he said. "It's a precaution."

"Seriously?" Yes, he'd had possessed people walking around the police station, but this was not a helpful way to identify one. Not least because he'd *brought* me here. "Wouldn't it be easier if I talked to an animal? Demons can't do that."

"What if you were possessed and didn't know it?"

"You've officially lost your minds." I backed away, the automatic doors sliding open again. "I'm not getting involved in this."

"Sorry, Robin," said a voice from behind me. "You might want to close your eyes."

The strong smell of sage filled my nostrils and stung my eyes, causing me to squeeze them shut for a moment. When I opened them again, I found someone had thrown sage all over me *and* Ramsey. Not to mention my lunch.

"Thanks for that, Seth," I said to the culprit, ruefully eyeing my latte. "Anyone want their coffee with extra sage?"

Seth grinned as he sidled past. The tall Black man was pretty much the only officer in the building I got along with, and as one of the people who'd been possessed by a demon, it was understandable that he'd taken to carrying a bag of sage in his pockets, same as me. The difference was, I didn't typically throw it into people's faces.

Ramsey eyed Seth in exasperation. "You might have suggested that sooner."

"You mean the sage?" I asked. "Isn't it obvious that it's way more efficient than bombarding people with security questions?"

"I thought so too." Seth gave me a wave and walked towards one of the back rooms, while Ramsey picked sage out of his hair.

"Happy now?" I said to my brother and Julian both. "Now, are you going to tell me why you put me through that nonsense?"

In answer, Ramsey led me across the lobby to his office, where he closed the door behind us. As usual, the small room was pristine, without so much as a single paper out of place. Prickles the hedgehog sat demurely in the middle of the clean desk, wearing an expression as stern as his owner's.

Ramsey's manner showed a touch of weariness as he stepped behind the desk to face me. "I had a call from Araminta's neighbour. She got attacked by slugs."

"The curse hit her too?" Did that constitute an emergency worth involving the police in? "Does she know that Araminta might be responsible?"

"She didn't say," he said, "but I told her the Head Witch would go to her house after work to deal with the problem."

"You said *what?*" I spluttered. "It's not my job to help with people's gardens. At this rate, they'll start asking me to help with the weeding as well."

"It *is* your job to take an active interest in the matters of the coven."

I raised my hands. "All right. It's not like I didn't spend half the weekend helping Mum, but if this is going to be an ongoing problem, finding the cause is more productive than removing the slugs one at a time."

"There's no reason you can't do both."

"I thought detective work was *your* job," I said. "Also, Araminta would love for everyone to become fixated on her and forget everything else, wouldn't she?"

"This isn't just about Araminta," he said. "I have a suspicion that this curse is more than it seems."

"That's called 'paranoia,' Ramsey," I told him. "Remember the demons? The ones scheming against me? They'll have a field day when they figure out that we're distracted by a vindictive witch and a bunch of slugs."

"Anything involving curses is a potential threat to our

safety," he said. "Besides, I would have thought you'd take an interest. You usually do."

"I didn't know Araminta. I don't know who killed her, assuming someone did at all." It wasn't like Ramsey to jump to conclusions, nor Mum either. "Unless there's something the pair of you aren't telling me, there's no reason to make me waste my time with this. Mum said she left the Reaper a message. That seems more pertinent."

"She did," he said, "but until she receives a reply, the best thing you can do is get on with your job."

"Which is not a slug exterminator." If Mum had her way, she'd have me de-slugging everyone's gardens until sundown. *Honestly.* "I'm going back to the office."

After I left the police station, I gave my sage-flavoured latte to the local pigeons, who appreciated it more than I did, and then went to buy a new one from Rowan before I went back to work.

I'd hoped for an update from the Reaper that afternoon, but none came. Regardless, Mum had "borrowed" Chloe again, which left me to deal with Grandma's antics all afternoon, and after another practice session with the sceptre, I wasn't feeling particularly charitable towards her by the end of the day.

As the workday closed, I went to find Tansy. She came scampering up to join me at the back door to the coven's headquarters. "Is there a reason your mother is storing buckets of slugs in the maze?"

"I wondered where she'd put them." If the Henbane Coven went snooping over the fence, they'd get a surprise. "You know, I forgot about the Henbanes. Do you think *they* might have had a role in this slug business?"

"Are there any Henbanes left to set a curse loose against us?" Tansy queried. "I don't think so. If Leona came back, she'd do worse than terrorise people's gardens."

True. Leona, a magical dud, had made a deal with a demon and let it possess her. I didn't know if she was even still alive at this point. Demons relied upon humans to get around, feeding on their life energy. Creepy as hell.

Tansy jumped onto my shoulder. "Where're we going? Home?"

"I wish." I sighed inwardly. "Ramsey volunteered me to clean up Araminta's neighbour's garden."

"Ramsey did that?" Tansy said. "What's got into him?"

"The same thing that's possessed Mum… Maybe not the best word to use," I added with a slight shiver. They *had* been possessed by demons, and maybe I was being unfair in expecting them to go back to normal immediately afterwards. "Mum also said she was planning to set up a meeting with the local Reaper."

Tansy hunched up smaller. "That's what you wanted, right?"

"In theory." Meeting the Reaper would bring me one step closer to fulfilling the mission the sceptre had given me, but despite all the practising I'd done, I didn't feel any readier to face the demons again. The trouble was, demons were literally invincible, and even banishing them to the deeper afterworld wasn't a permanent solution, as my grandmother had discovered. Winning myself a couple of decades of breathing room was the best I could expect, but even that seemed insurmountable at the moment.

Once the task was complete, though, I wouldn't have to wield the sceptre any longer. I'd be free.

With Tansy on my shoulder, I walked to Mum's office and knocked on the door. The murmur of voices quietened, and Mum opened the door. "Robin. I thought you'd left."

"Ramsey wants me to clean up Araminta's neighbour's garden," I told her. "I assumed you knew."

"Yes, we'll go there at once." She nodded to Chloe. "You can leave."

Suspicion prickled at me. "Is there a reason the two of you have spent most of the day working together? Something I should know?"

"Really, Robin. Not everything is a conspiracy."

"Tell Ramsey that," I said. "He has his receptionist interrogating anyone who tries to walk into the police station in case they're possessed."

Mum pursed her lips. "He's trying his best to deal with a difficult situation. You could stand to be a little more cooperative."

"How is removing slugs from people's gardens remotely relevant?" I shook my head. "Why would Leona bother with that when she could set a flesh-eating monster loose on me instead?"

"This is no laughing matter." Mum strode out of her office and closed the door behind her. "We'll help Araminta's neighbour. Don't forget she's the one who found Araminta's body, so she might know more about the circumstances of her death."

"All right, but if you and Chloe are setting me up to volunteer as the next flower club leader, I'd sooner let the demons have me instead."

"I don't like slugs," Tansy said into my ear as we walked out of the coven's headquarters. "I'm going home."

"I'll see you there." I didn't blame her for wanting to avoid Mum in her current mood, but I wished I had her with me for moral support while Mum and I walked back to Araminta's cottage.

This time, Mum made for the neighbouring door instead.

"The witch who lives here is called Dawn," she told me in an undertone. "She's retired, and she's also the one who found Araminta's body."

"I know, and she called the police to report that her garden was full of slugs," I added. "Does that suggest she knows where they came from?"

"It might," she said, "but let me speak to her first."

"If you like." Warily, I stood back while Mum knocked on the door.

A red-haired witch dressed in voluminous green robes answered, and typically, her attention went straight to my sceptre. "Head Witch. And... Lady Wildwood. To what do I owe the pleasure?"

"You requested help cleaning your garden," Mum replied. "We've come to assist."

Her other brow crept up. "I assumed the police were using you as an excuse to get rid of me. I didn't think you'd show up."

"The Head Witch always takes the opportunity to check up on her fellow witches," Mum told her.

*The Head Witch wishes she was on another planet.* "Out of curiosity, why call the police and not the coven?"

"I did call the coven," said Dawn. "They told me to stop wasting their time."

"Was that Aunt—ah, Shannon Wildwood by any chance?" I asked, forgetting Mum's order to let her do all the talking herself.

"Yes," she said, "it was. If you're volunteering to help, though, I certainly won't object."

Mum and I entered the house, which was laid out in the same manner as Araminta's cottage next door, with a large glass window at the back overlooking the garden. Dawn's garden was a tad more restrained than her neighbour's, though part of that was due to the abundance of glistening black slugs covering every plant within sight.

"They're normal sized," I whispered to Mum. "I wonder

why the ones at the match were the only ones that blew up into giants."

Mum ignored me and got to work. Wand in hand, she cast transportation spells on each group of slugs, while I joined her, wondering if there was a limit to how much those buckets would hold. What if they escaped into the coven's garden? Assuming the coven wasn't next on the list already, I could only imagine how many extra tedious coven meetings would ensue. Aunt Shannon would doubtless find a way to make the infestation my fault if she hadn't already.

As I sent the last group of slugs packing, Mum addressed Dawn. "You were the one who found Araminta, weren't you?"

"Yes, I was," she replied. "I wouldn't have seen her if not for the sparks."

"What sparks?" I asked curiously.

"Bright-pink ones," she replied. "Cast by a wand, I assume. I saw them floating above the fence, and when I looked through the hedge, I saw her lying on the path."

Weird. "Did she cast the spell herself? Or someone else?"

"There wasn't anyone else there," she said. "It's odd… Was fine the last time I saw her."

"When was that?" I could tell Mum wasn't happy about me taking over the questioning, but Dawn struck me less and less like a potential killer with every word she said.

"Oh, she was always out in the garden," she replied. "I saw her almost every day. Well, heard her, from the other side of that giant hedge of hers. Talking to herself, you know."

"Was she always alone?"

"Certainly. She liked her privacy." She lifted her head. "Oh, that's a pretty squirrel."

I swivelled to the fence. A red squirrel sat on the fence between the gardens, its bright-red fur shining under the sinking sun. Not Tansy.

"Hey." I stepped in that direction. "You were at the Sky Hopper game. Who are you?"

The squirrel vanished over the fence in a flash of fluffy tail. Mum gave me a sharp look that said she'd skewer me with my own sceptre if I tried to climb the fence, but an alarming screeching came from Araminta's garden, followed by a familiar squeak. "YOU!"

"Tansy!" Oh no. She must have followed me after all. Stifling curses, I ran back through Dawn's house and out the front then used my wand to unlock Araminta's door.

In the back garden, Tansy and the squirrel grappled with one another on the lawn in a blur of red fur and claws.

"Whoa." I didn't quite dare get involved in case I got my face clawed off. "Tansy—stop that."

Mum caught up to me, her expression incandescent. "Robin, that is *enough*."

I might have pointed out that I wasn't the one engaged in a wrestling match, but I was starting to worry that they might do one another serious damage.

"Stop that!" I pointed the sceptre, intending to aim at the intruder alone, but they were tumbling over one another so quickly that my freezing charm caused both squirrels to stop midmotion. "Ah."

Tansy would not be thrilled with me, but it couldn't be helped. I picked up my familiar with my free hand and moved her away from the other squirrel before casting a reversal charm. To my intense relief, the spell worked, and Tansy jumped to her feet.

My familiar shook herself. "You froze me!"

"I was aiming for the other squirrel," I told her. "You were moving too fast. Did you follow me here?"

"No, I followed *him*," she said indignantly. "He was sniffing around our garden."

"Was he?" I glanced at Mum, whose manner suggested she

wanted to turn *me* into a statue next. "Tansy, he can't speak for himself as long as he's frozen. If I undo the spell, will you agree not to try to strangle him while I ask him some questions?"

Tansy pouted. "Fine."

I flicked the sceptre, unfreezing the other squirrel, and cast a levitation charm a heartbeat later. The squirrel bounced into the air like he was on a trampoline, and I shot out a hand and caught him by the tail.

"Let me go!" he yelled, while I grinned to myself. A few short weeks ago, casting *one* spell with the sceptre had been beyond me, much less two spells one after another. Not that Mum was rushing to offer me praise.

"Nice try," I told the squirrel. Up close, it was clear he was male, slightly bigger than Tansy, and presumably the same squirrel who'd been at the match. The odds of *two* showing up were less than zero. I held him up to eye level, looking into his beady little eyes. "Why were you nosing around my mother's garden?"

"None of your beeswax." He lifted his chin. "*You* must be one of the Wildwoods."

"He knows who you are!" Tansy said. "He *has* been spying on us."

"That and I can understand him," I reminded her. "Who *doesn't* know who I am? The question is, who are *you*?"

"I am Radcliffe," he said self-importantly. "My witch, Nasturtium—"

"What kind of a name is that?" Tansy cracked up laughing, while the other squirrel squirmed in the air, trying to reach her.

"Tansy." To the other squirrel—Radcliffe—I added, "Who is your witch?"

He continued to flail around. "She won't let you get away with this!"

"Where is she, then?" Tansy goaded him. "At home?"

"Certainly not," he growled. "She's coming here to collect her inheritance."

"Inheritance?" Then… Oh no. She must be related to Araminta.

6

When I lowered the squirrel to the ground, he took off like a rocket. Tansy pelted after him in pursuit, far too fast for me to keep up, and I resignedly turned to Mum's irked face.

"The squirrel belongs to one of Araminta's relatives," I said before she could take me to task for Tansy's actions. "Isn't it worth talking to him?"

Mum's eyes narrowed. "Absolutely not. I won't have rodents brawling on our property."

"I thought you wanted to investigate Araminta's death." I kept my voice low in case Dawn was listening in, though it didn't look as though she'd followed Mum into Araminta's house.

"None of Araminta's relatives were here when she died, Robin," she said. "They aren't suspects."

"That squirrel showed up at the Sky Hopper game the same day as her death, though," I pointed out. "I'm not saying I think he was involved—or his owner—but I think it's worth asking some questions. Also, her relatives might know more about this curse of hers and how we can stop it."

Mum swept away into the house. "I thought you weren't interested in helping with the curse."

"I never said that." I followed her through the living room. "I thought you *were* interested, and we do need to stop the curse. How long before you run out of space to store magically created slugs in the coven's garden?"

"Chloe and I are working on a strategy," she said. "That, Robin, is what we were discussing earlier."

"Okay, keep your hair on." My phone pinged in my pocket. Harvey, I guessed. "I should go and find Tansy."

She gave me a long-suffering look. "All right, but you'd better not run off into the forest if that's where she went."

She *might* have if she'd been determined enough to catch the other squirrel to run past the safety of the wall of sage the police had put around the forest immediately behind my mother's house, but I seized on the chance to escape my mother before she found another slug-infested garden to drag me into.

I checked my phone and found that Harvey had messaged, asking if I wanted to meet at the Fox's Den. I replied saying yes, mentally prepared to fight another battle with my mother or Ramsey, and returned home in a considerably improved mood.

At my mother's house, I found Tansy waiting on the front garden wall. "Did the squirrel escape?"

"Yes." She huffed. "Only because I let him go. I could have caught him easily."

"Uh-huh." I spied Mum approaching out of the corner of my eye. "Want to come to the Fox's Den?"

"Only if you buy me some peanuts."

"The staff always give them to you anyway, you know that." To Mum, I added, "I'm going to the Fox's Den with Harvey."

To my relief, Mum didn't offer anything more than a sigh

and a "don't stay out too late." She seemed to have lost her drive to micromanage my life, at least for the time being.

While I did have to explain the latest fiasco to Harvey, it was nice to have a normal, drama-free meal at the pub with my boyfriend amid the chaos of the past few days.

"I thought there was something odd about those slugs," he remarked when I'd explained the origin of the trouble at the Sky Hopper game. "What did Araminta have against Sky Hopper?"

"The pitch is where the flower contest took place."

"Ah." He picked up his beer glass. "Araminta cursed every single person who wronged her to be plagued with slugs? That's harsh."

"Apparently," I replied. "Not sure how she pulled it off, given that the curse outlasted her death. Mum is the expert, not me, and Ramsey's the one who's supposed to solve murders, so I don't know why they're insisting on dragging me into this."

"Murders." His eyes widened. "Your brother thinks the flower club leader was murdered?"

"He and Mum have started the Society for Irrational Paranoia." I sipped my drink. "Nah, I'm being unfair. They both got possessed by a demon, which makes them entitled to be on edge, and Araminta was unpleasant enough that it's not out of the realm of possibility that someone bumped her off. I'm just lost on why they think this is remotely relevant to my mission as Head Witch."

"How's that going, anyway?"

I pulled a face. "I managed to unfreeze a couple of squirrels using my sceptre, so I guess you could say I'm improving my technique."

"Only because you *froze* me in the first place." Tansy flicked her tail into my drink, splashing me in the face.

Harvey blinked. "Two squirrels?"

"Yeah, there was another red squirrel sniffing around, and Tansy took offence."

"Whose squirrel?" He eyed Tansy. "Red squirrels aren't all that common. Someone's familiar?"

"One of Araminta's relatives, allegedly." I rolled my eyes. "The squirrel legged it, but Mum decided it's not worth pursuing. Don't ask why. She was happy to volunteer me to remove slugs from people's gardens."

"Seems a bit degrading for the Head Witch."

"I thought so too." I shrugged. "Between that and my brother insisting on asking security questions of anyone who comes into the police station to make sure they aren't possessed by a demon, I'm starting to think that they're both losing their minds."

"If Araminta was murdered, it's bound to have him worried," he said. "You don't think the demons might have been involved, do you?"

"Nope," I said. "Not a chance. Araminta had a huge list of enemies. Possibly a literal one."

"And they're all being plagued with slugs," he concluded. "What did you end up doing with the slugs, anyway?"

"Right now, they're sitting in buckets in the coven's garden," I replied. "I know, it's not ideal. We need to find the cause, but I'm slightly run off my feet at the moment."

"I bet," he said. "Ah—I forgot to ask. The photos you took during the match. Have you still got them?"

"The photos." I slapped my forehead. "Yes. I do. Sorry I forgot to send them to you."

"You've had a lot on your mind. We all have."

"I'll sort the photos later and send you any good ones," I replied. "I should have done that as soon as I got back from the match."

"Really, it's no problem." He reached out across the table

and gave my hand a reassuring squeeze. "I didn't mean to add to your stress. There's no rush."

"Exactly." Tansy hopped onto my shoulder and wrapped her tail around my neck. "Stop beating yourself up. Your family does a good enough job of that already."

I lowered my gaze. "They were getting better. Then... the demons."

"It's a huge ask for *anyone* to deal with what you have to." He knotted his fingers in mine. "Really, Robin, you're doing great."

My eyes stung with unexpected tears. "I'm trying, but that's never been enough for my family, and now... I have no idea what they want from me."

My argument with Ramsey before the Sky Hopper match came rushing back, tearing at my heart. Even if I achieved the seemingly impossible and dealt with the demons then surrendered the sceptre to its rightful wielder, would that be enough? Would I still be pushed into making a choice that would drive me away from here?

"They should want for you to choose your own destiny," Harvey said. "If not... Well, I'll always back you up. So will your dad, and Piper, and Rowan, and plenty of other people in your life."

I blinked again, hard. "It's not that easy for coven leaders or Head Witches. It sounds like I'm making excuses for them, I know, but the rest of the coven isn't making matters easier. The council is a nightmare on a good day, and frankly, I'd like to see *them* set up a meeting with a Reaper."

He released my hand. "You have a meeting with a Reaper?"

"If he ever answers the phone." I picked up the menu and ordered another drink. "It shouldn't be *that* hard to find someone who can pretty much teleport from one place to another, but that also makes him hard to pin down. From what Maura told me, Reapers aren't big into modern technology, either."

"Tricky." He ordered a drink too. "It's hardly your fault, though. I just wish there was something I could do to help."

"Just being here is enough." My mood had improved already, though I felt bad that our dates always seemed to involve me venting about my incorrigible family. "I need some normality in my life. At this rate, I'll have to answer security questions just to enter my own house. A house, I might add, that I never wanted to live in again."

He stiffened. "You still want to leave… after?"

I'd spoken without thinking, and regret hit me like an out-of-control broomstick. *Did* I want to leave? For him, I wanted to stay, but I couldn't reconcile that need with the impulse to run for the hills before it was no longer an option.

"I… don't know," I hedged. "I have a hard time thinking about after this is all over, to be honest. I'm taking it one day at a time."

"I understand."

Shame burned my cheeks. He'd announced his intention to support me wholeheartedly, and I'd responded by implying I'd sooner walk into a volcano than stay at his side. I wished I could offer him a reassurance, but I wouldn't just be making the choice for myself. By remaining in Wildwood Heath, I'd implicitly back up the expectations that my brother had voiced during our argument. That I was bound to settle down—emphasis on *settle*—and never stray from my family's path again.

*Settling down.* I really hated those words. Even if they accepted Harvey as the person I'd chosen, how could I ever be happy knowing that any potential children I had would be chained to the same expectations as I'd been? I couldn't do that to another person.

"I… need a new job for a start," I said in a clumsy attempt

to change the subject. "If there are vacancies open to former delivery people who also had a brief stint as a Head Witch. At least my CV is memorable."

He cracked a smile, seizing on the change of subject. "That's true. You'll always be guaranteed an interview."

We talked of more pleasant topics for the remainder of the night, yet the tension remained in the background, and we lapsed into silence as we walked home. Even when he kissed me goodnight, I sensed the unspoken words simmering beneath the surface.

"I'll send the photos," I promised, darting into the house before I started babbling and dug myself into a deeper hole than I already had.

If Mum and Ramsey had waited up for me, I didn't see them. I made straight for the stairs to my room, where I dug out my camera to go through the photos from the match.

"I can't believe I forgot," I muttered to myself.

"I can." Tansy hopped onto my bedside table. "You're determined to beat yourself up over this, aren't you? Why?"

"I know it's not the first time I've forgotten something important." That was part of the problem. The accumulated failures piled up, and while none of my decisions as Head Witch in the past week fell into the "failure" category, I'd hardly been a shining success, either.

Tansy flicked me on the nose with her tail. "Harvey doesn't care! He'll support you even if you want to become a professional Pokémon trainer."

"I wish." I'd actually had a part-time job at a magical zoo once, but after one too many arguments with idiotic wizards who'd tried to take a selfie with a manticore and almost caused a stampede, I'd decided any public-facing role wasn't for me. "Okay… let's see if there are any clues hidden in these pictures."

I skimmed through the photos and selected which ones to

print. As I'd expected, the crowd was out of focus in the majority of the photos, and the red squirrel was a blur of colour, nothing more. I hadn't caught a snap of his owner, so I'd have to wait until Araminta's relative showed up in town before I delved any further into the possibility that the pair of them had played a role in the slug incident.

Or her murder.

———

I slept like crap that night, weighted down by guilt over my outburst at my date with Harvey and my general discontent with my family members. The next morning, I poured myself a huge mug of coffee while Tansy hopped onto the breakfast table and yawned. She'd been patrolling the garden all night as though she'd thought the other squirrel would materialise and steal all her sunflower seeds, though there'd been no sign of him since the previous day.

Ramsey, who sat opposite me, eyed Tansy in disapproval. "What's all this about another squirrel?"

"Did Mum tell you he belongs to one of Araminta's relatives?" I poured cereal into a bowl. "I'm not sure why, but she didn't think it's worth questioning them."

"That's not what she told me." His mouth turned down at the corners. "I've asked the staff at the Owl's Nest inn to inform me if someone by the name Nasturtium checks into a room there."

"Wait, Mum's gone from ignoring Araminta's relatives to stalking them?"

"I'd see that squirrel coming a mile off," Tansy announced. "I don't trust him."

"You look like you're about to doze off," I pointed out. "Ramsey, do you want me to come to the police station after work?"

I'd rather walk there myself than have him show up at the café again, though I drew the line at answering any more ridiculous security questions.

"Do that" was his reply.

A snore from Tansy told me she'd fallen asleep. *It's all right for some people.* I, however, had another joyous day of paperwork and spell practise with Grandma ahead of me, though at least there was no council meeting this afternoon. Small mercies.

When I reached the office, I found Grandma levitating stacks of paperwork above my desk while humming under her breath.

"What're you doing?" I propped a hand on my hip. "Unless you're planning on filling out those forms by yourself, put them back where you found them."

"I'll do it," Chloe offered, pointing her wand at the papers and levitating them back onto the desk.

Shooting her a look of gratitude, I moved behind the desk and faced my grandmother's ghost. "Grandma, if you're sad about Araminta, you can talk about it, you know."

"Sad?" She gave a loud, false laugh. "Everyone knows death is just the beginning."

"Have you seen her ghost yet?" I asked suspiciously.

"No, but I expect she'll show up soon enough," she said. "I'll give her the tour."

"Of the afterworld?" *Please, not my office.* I didn't need *two* cranky elderly ghosts flitting around the place. "It's been three days since she died. That means if she's going to show up, it'll be today."

"Or tonight." She grinned. "Do you want me to come to the house and tell you?"

"Not on your life. Or afterlife." Grandma could *almost* reach the house, but her ghostly wandering had its limits, and luckily, she hadn't managed to get inside yet. It'd spell the end of any semblance of peace I had when she did.

Since Mum hadn't monopolised Chloe today, we got through all the necessary paperwork in a timely manner for once. Non–coven meeting days always went faster, and while I dropped in on Rowan at lunchtime, I steered clear of the police station until after work.

When I left my office at the day's end, Mum was waiting beside the front door. "I heard from Ramsey," she told me. "He said that Nasturtium did indeed check into the inn earlier today and that she intended to go to her mother's house."

"Her *mother*." That was the squirrel's owner? Araminta's daughter?

"Precisely." She beckoned to me. "I think we should speak to her ourselves."

"You think she's a suspect?" I went to the coven's garden to look for Tansy, but she was nowhere to be seen. At a guess, she must have stayed at home to keep an eye out for more squirrel-shaped intruders.

Mum waited for me by the door with visible impatience and then took off at a fast stride as soon as I caught up. I followed her out of the coven headquarters towards the main street, clutching the sceptre in my hand. "Mum, Ramsey doesn't have proof it was murder yet. Or does he?"

"Not that I'm aware of."

"Then Nasturtium has no reason to answer our questions," I pointed out. "What're you going to do, offer your condolences?"

"It worked well enough with the others, didn't it?"

"I guess." I dropped my voice when we passed a group of wizards who must have been on their way home from work, all of whom goggled at my sceptre. "Ah—did the Reaper ever answer your message?"

Her jaw twitched. "No. He didn't."

"Maybe he's taken a holiday." Unlikely. From what I'd heard, Reapers cared about one thing—their jobs—and everything else was secondary. Really, they weren't all that different from certain family members of mine. Not that either would appreciate the comparison.

Turning into the cul-de-sac where Araminta had lived, Mum peered through the gap in the living room curtains. "Yes… there's someone in there."

At her knock, a thirty-something woman with a younger copy of Araminta's sneering face answered the door. "Yes?"

"You must be Nasturtium," said Mum. "Araminta's daughter."

"And *you're* Lady Wildwood." She had one of those voices that sounded like she perpetually had a lemon in her mouth, and an expression to match. "And the Head Witch. Here to swindle me out of my inheritance, are you?"

"No. What would make you think that?" I'd have thought she'd know the Wildwoods had enough money of their own.

"It's what everyone else wants," she said sniffily. "Yes, they show up here and offer condolences, but I know better."

*Okay…* "I don't need your inheritance," I told her. "As a matter of fact, we're here to ask whether your mother set a curse to go into effect after her death."

Mum stiffened, but a grin crept across Nasturtium's face. "Did she now? Which did she go with in the end, frogs or slugs?"

"Slugs." Now we were getting somewhere. "Did she tell you everything? Including which people she was going to curse?"

"Yes, she wrote a list," said Nasturtium. "She might have updated it since the last time, but I have a copy somewhere."

"She gave you a copy?" Had she really made it that easy?

"Why, did she spend a lot of time contemplating her own death?"

Mum scowled at me, but Nasturtium laughed again. "She didn't have many hobbies except for her garden. Yes, I heard about the flower contest too. It wouldn't surprise me if she put everyone responsible for that fiasco at the top of her list."

"The curse started in the same field as the flower contest," I acknowledged. "Then it hit a few people's gardens, including the other flower club members' and her neighbour's."

"How delightful." Her face was radiant enough that you'd think she'd just won the lottery. "Pity I missed it."

*Your familiar didn't.*

Mum stepped in before I could speak. "When did you arrive in Wildwood Heath?"

"I got here today, of course," she replied. "Do you want to see that list? I know where she kept it."

"You do?" This I had to see. "Sure."

Nasturtium went back into the house, but Mum caught my arm before I could enter through the closing door. "Robin, be careful," she hissed in my ear.

"She's lying," I breathed. "Her familiar... He was definitely at the match. There aren't that many red squirrels around."

"Don't say a word," she ordered. "This woman might be dangerous."

"All right, keep your hair on." I tugged my sleeve free and waited for Araminta's daughter to return.

Soon, Nasturtium emerged from the house with a piece of paper in her outstretched hand and a wide smile on her face. "Yes... here it is."

Mum held out a hand to take the paper, while I peered over her shoulder. I couldn't read all the words in Araminta's cramped handwriting, but I recognised a few names. "Dawn... and... Lady Wildwood?"

Mum gave no reaction to her name. "No doubt she moved me up the list after the incident with the flower contest, but my garden is quite safe."

Sensing the need for a change of subject, I addressed Nasturtium. "Curses usually stop working when the caster dies. Do you know how she managed to get around that rule?"

"She put the curse on an object, I assume," she said cheerfully. "No doubt she picked something nobody would suspect. I have to give her credit for inventiveness."

"An object... like this list?" I gestured at the paper in Mum's hands. "If that's the case, I think the police ought to have a look at it."

Nasturtium's mouth tightened. "Now, you must understand this was entirely my mother's work. I had nothing to do with it."

*We'll see.* "Where's your familiar?"

Her smile slipped. "Familiar? What familiar?"

"Your—" I hissed out a breath when Mum trod on my foot, subtly enough to make it look like an accident, and pushed the list of names into my hand.

"We'll come back later," Mum said to Nasturtium. "Thanks for the help."

Araminta's daughter closed the door on us while I rubbed my sore foot with the hand that held the paper. "What was that in aid of?"

"Give that to your brother." She indicated the paper and began walking away at speed.

I followed her out of the cul-de-sac, where she veered towards home. "I'd like to see Tansy before I go to the police station. She was looking for that squirrel."

Mum clucked her teeth. "I doubt she found him if he's half as wily as she is."

True, but Tansy would want to know the recent development. When we reached the house, Mum unlocked the front door and went in, while I called my familiar.

Tansy appeared on the fence and came scampering up to me. "Where've you been?"

"Araminta's house," I replied. "Have you seen that squirrel?"

"No," she growled. "Why, did he show up at Araminta's house again?"

"No, but I bet he will, given that his owner's there." I waved the list. "Araminta's daughter. She also found this list of people who're going to be cursed, so I'm going to take this to Ramsey. Want to come?"

"What kind of question is that?" Tansy bounded into action. "Bring it on."

"She wrote a list of people she planned to curse?" Tansy snickered when I'd finished telling her the latest news. "And your mum thinks she cursed the paper?"

"Yes." I glanced down at the paper clutched in my hand. "I guess it's too late for me if the curse can be passed on by touch, but I don't think it can."

Somehow, Araminta had engineered the curse so that it only affected the people on the list. It must have taken weeks of preparation, but that was perfectly doable for someone with a burning grudge and an unlimited amount of free time on their hands.

When we entered the police station, my brother ambushed me at the door. "Stop right there."

"Not this again." I swivelled to the desk in the hopes that Julian would come to my rescue, but the receptionist didn't look up from his paperwork. "Doesn't anyone have any sage?"

"No," Ramsey said. "We used it all."

"By throwing it on your fellow officers?" I surmised. "If I

was a demon, I'd be able to instantly anticipate any question you might ask. Isn't there a better way to check if someone's possessed? There must be."

"Most of the methods would involve throwing you out of windows," Ramsey said testily. "I trust you wouldn't enjoy that."

"Throwing me out of windows?" I bit back a surprised laugh. "That was almost a joke, Ramsey. Are you feeling okay?"

"Just answer the security question," he said snippily. "How old were you when you first left home?"

"Eighteen, and a demon might have known the same." I rolled my eyes. "Can I come in now?"

"Not yet." He turned to Tansy. "You have to answer one too."

"I am not possessed by a demon! I am a squirrel!" Tansy squeaked indignantly.

"Ramsey, this is too much," I said. "Familiars can't get possessed. You know that."

His jaw twitched. "Fine."

Tansy and I followed him into his office, where I held out the list of names. "I got this from Nasturtium, Araminta's daughter. She found it in her mother's house. Turns out Araminta listed out her worst enemies, so we can make a reasonable guess as to who's going to be plagued by slugs next."

"A list of the curse's targets?" He didn't take the paper from me. "Are you sure the paper isn't cursed?"

"Bit late if it is." I dropped the paper on the desk. "I'm not going to turn into a slug, Ramsey. That's not what the curse does."

Tansy jumped onto the desk too. "If the paper's cursed, can't you just rip it up? Or burn it?"

"There's no guarantee that would work," Ramsey replied. "No... we'll need a specialised curse-breaker to look at it."

"Do you know one?"

A knock on Ramsey's office door interrupted his reply.

"Yes?" he called.

Seth pushed open the door. "Sorry to intrude, but I just got a call from the hospital. Turns out... Araminta was poisoned."

*She was poisoned?* I stared at Ramsey, whose jaw tightened. "Robin, you should leave."

I gestured to the paper. "Do you want to keep this, or...?"

"No, I think our mother can make better use of it than I can."

"You didn't even *read* the list," I said ineffectually. "All right, if you're sure."

Seth gave me an apologetic look as I walked past him on my way out of the office, my mind whirling. Araminta *had* been murdered. My family's paranoia wasn't unjustified, and on top of the curse turning out to be genuine, I'd be eating my own words for a while yet.

"Does Mum know any curse-breakers?" I muttered to Tansy as we walked down the high street. "Or does she plan to try to break the curse herself?"

"Your guess is as good as mine." She scampered alongside me. "Poison. I wonder how they did it. Araminta rarely went out except into her garden."

"And flower club meetings," I added, thinking of the thorn-killer-toxin incident. "It's lucky they don't meet at the café anymore."

"She dropped dead at home," Tansy said. "That suggests someone slipped the poison into her drink or food inside her own house. A person could have been spotted, but a small animal might have slipped in."

I frowned, figuring I knew what she was getting at. "She'd have noticed an animal intruder."

"Squirrels can be stealthy." She slowed her pace and moved her paws carefully in demonstration. "I could slip poison into someone's drink when their back was turned without being noticed."

"Please don't say that in front of Ramsey. He'd take it as a confession." I turned the corner of the street. "Weird that Nasturtium denied having a familiar. Mum didn't let me ask any more questions, though."

"I bet that squirrel has been hiding since I ambushed him," Tansy said smugly. "He's terrified of me."

"Uh-huh." I slowed, seeing Mum outside the front door of the house. *Here we go.*

She beckoned me over. "Robin, I need your help."

"With what?" I held out the list of names. "Ramsey said we needed to find a curse-breaker."

"Not yet," she said. "The slugs at the coven headquarters escaped."

Uh-oh. "Into the maze?"

"Everywhere." On that ominous note, she swept down the road towards the covens' headquarters, clearly expecting me to follow.

Tansy twitched her tail. "I'm going to find that squirrel. I bet he had something to do with this."

"If you say so." Bracing myself, I followed my mother's lead. I rolled up the list of names and tucked it into my pocket as I walked into the coven's headquarters and through the lobby.

Mum hadn't been kidding about the state of the garden. The lawn was covered in slugs, oozing over every flower. Strangely enough, none of them had climbed the fence to the Henbane Coven's headquarters, but their garden was in a sorry enough state already, without any greenery save for a few dismal-looking weeds.

"About time you showed up." Aunt Shannon came marching over, her wand held aloft. "This is unacceptable."

"Why are you still at work?" I lifted my sceptre, though I didn't quite dare cast a levitation spell with her in the vicinity in case I accidentally hit her as well as the slugs. However amusing the mental image might be, it wouldn't be worth the backlash.

"I thought you'd gone home," Mum said to her. "Move aside. Robin will handle this."

Surprise rose within me at her proclamation, but Aunt Shannon didn't budge. "I don't remember asking you to give me orders."

She gave a sharp flick of her wand. A loud bang went off, and several slugs flew into the air, only to fall back onto the grass again.

"They're magically conjured, I told you," Mum said. "The result of a curse. They can't be destroyed or disappeared."

"Why did you store them in the coven's garden, then?" Aunt Shannon tutted. "Foolish, if you ask me."

*Yeah, right.* Had *she* "accidentally" let them out? It wouldn't surprise me, but it'd been inevitable that some of them would eventually escape from the buckets where Mum had stashed them.

Mum strode around her sister and waved her wand, causing several buckets to glide towards us from the maze.

Taking my cue, I pointed the sceptre at the nearest group of slugs, levitating them into one of the buckets. As I moved to the next, Aunt Shannon retreated into the coven's headquarters and left Mum and me to deal with the rest.

"Was it her, do you think?" I whispered to Mum, waving the sceptre again. "I bet she set them loose in the garden."

No response came, but her jaw tightened. I got on with

helping levitate slugs off the grass until the buckets were full and Mum was able to return them to the maze.

"We can't leave them here indefinitely, can we?" I peered at her face, which remained inscrutable. "We have to find a permanent solution. Ramsey suggested getting a curse-breaker to look at that list in case that's what she put the curse on, which might be worth a try."

"We'll discuss this later." Mum shot a meaningful look in the direction of the coven headquarters, where Aunt Shannon watched through the back door. *She's still here?*

When we walked back into the lobby, Aunt Shannon surveyed me. "Pity those slugs weren't demons."

I stiffened. "Excuse me?"

Her smile widened. "You heard me, didn't you, Robin? If those slugs were demons… Well, you handled *them*, didn't you?"

"What's that supposed to mean?"

She wasn't supposed to know about Grandma's demons, nor the reason I'd been given the sceptre in the first place, but it was kind of hard to avoid discussing the subject in public places, and her magpie familiar was notorious for eavesdropping.

Mum swept past her. "If you want to make yourself useful, Shannon, you'll help me contact local curse-breakers."

"Surely, the Head Witch can handle a harmless curse." Her eyes glittered with amusement. "It reflects terribly on our image when our supposed leader is so inept."

Time to drop the pretence. "What do you want?"

"What do I want?" She raised a brow. "I simply have concerns that you aren't fit to fulfil the task you were given. Cursed or not, slugs are considerably less difficult to deal with than demons, wouldn't you say?"

Oh boy. She knew. However she'd figured it out didn't matter. If she took the information to the press… Wait, did it even matter? I had Clarice and Speck's number myself if I really wanted to get the last word in. No, the real danger was that she'd play directly into the demons' hands.

"Breaking curses is a little below my station," I told her. "Now, if *you're* offering to help, you might want to start by cleaning up the garden. I'm sure my mother would appreciate the assistance."

She gave a delicate laugh. "I, too, have more important matters to deal with… unless this incident is less benign than it seems, of course."

"That would depend on who set the slugs loose in the garden, wouldn't it?" I matched her polite tone and walked away before she could reel me into an argument with another belittling comment.

Mum was already walking away. "I told you not to provoke her, Robin."

"She *knows*," I hissed as the doors closed behind us. "What's the betting she'll blackmail me by threatening to tell the rest of the council I have demons after me?"

"She won't if she has any sense," she replied. "The sceptre made its choice. Challenging that decision would endanger the coven."

I had my doubts that Aunt Shannon would care if her own ambition outmatched her desire for a peaceful existence. "She's the one who set the slugs loose. You know that."

"That was little more than a petty rebellion," she said. "A plea for attention."

"And a reminder that I *can't* undo the curse," I added. "Also, Araminta was murdered. The police got a call from the hospital saying she died by poisoning."

"Poison?" Her tone showed no surprise. "Give me that list."

"I'm guessing Aunt Shannon isn't on it." I retrieved the list from my pocket and gave it to my mother. "She isn't a suspect, either."

Despite being a massive pain in my rear. She'd almost certainly been watching the slug situation to see how she could leverage the curse in her favour, but the knowledge that she was fully aware of the extent of the burden on my shoulders was a more concerning issue. Not that I could do anything about *that* either.

Mum scanned the paper. "As I thought, there's nothing here about how to *stop* the curse."

"Did you expect there to be?" Had she thought Araminta would be thoughtful enough to leave a list of instructions? "Would catching Araminta's murderer help undo the curse, do you think?"

"Not if the two aren't connected," she replied. "If Araminta set up the curse to activate after her death regardless of the circumstances, it wouldn't matter whether she died of natural causes or otherwise."

"Typical."

When we reached the house, Mum made a beeline for the back garden. She then dispatched a bewildered Piper to plant fast-growing spiky vines around the edges of the garden and then ordered me to cast a bunch of fresh security spells on top of that. It seemed like overkill to me, but I knew better than to argue with Mum when she was in this kind of mood.

Tansy did her part by chasing pigeons away from the bird feeder and prowling up and down the fences in search of enemies both squirrel and otherwise. When the spells were done, Mum went into the house, leaving Piper and me to catch a breather.

"You weren't kidding when you said she's grown paranoid," Piper whispered to me as she surveyed her new handiwork. A thick, impenetrable hedge circled the garden, bristling with spines. "Does she think the curse will strike here next?"

"If it does, I'm not sure if even all these security measures will be able to stop it," I admitted. "Curses are tricky, especially ones that aren't aimed at a single target. I'm pretty sure I slept through that class."

"Me too." She cracked a grin. "She mentioned the curse was probably cast on an object…"

"Or a place," I said. "I thought it might have been cast on the list of names, but paper is easily destroyed."

"List?" she echoed. "Oh, is that what that paper was?"

"Yeah, a list of Araminta's enemies."

Piper choked on a laugh. "Seriously?"

"Araminta's daughter found it in her house," I explained. "Helpful of her to leave a list of targets, but it's looking as if we need to find a curse-breaker to actually undo the curse."

"Helpful." Her brow furrowed. "Hmm. Not to sound as paranoid as Lady Wildwood, but what if it was a forgery?"

"You think her daughter faked the list?"

Piper shrugged. "I don't know. I never met her, but it seems like someone really wants you distracted. You *and* your mother."

My thoughts went back to Aunt Shannon. "You aren't wrong, but Araminta was murdered. The police confirmed it. Even if the curse wasn't her work, someone bumped her off."

Piper's mouth parted. "Ouch. After the flower contest, a dozen people wanted a piece of her, I bet."

"That's why she's almost certainly the one who instigated the curse." I watched Tansy prowl across the fence above the newly grown spiky bushes. "Not that I know *who* killed her. Ramsey shooed me out of the office when he got the news."

"I bet. He doesn't like people treading on his toes."

"No, but Mum seems to want me to do it anyway." I lowered my voice, though our only neighbour was Aunt

Shannon, and she already knew more than she should. "She doesn't even seem to care that Aunt Shannon decided to set the slugs loose in the coven's garden and make it look like an accident. And… and she knows about the mission the sceptre gave me."

"She *knows*?" Piper's eyes bulged. "Who told her?"

"Probably her familiar." I lowered my voice. "It was only a matter of time before she figured out why the sceptre chose me."

Piper wasn't supposed to know either, but it was kind of hard for someone to work inside my mother's house and not overhear enough snippets of our conversations to put two and two together. I was pretty sure Kimberly knew, too, but Mum had selected her staff because they were trustworthy. Aunt Shannon was a different story.

Piper swore. "When did she figure it out?"

"Right away, in all likelihood," I replied. "She has her magpie on high alert, so it was only a matter of time."

"I guess." Her gaze flickered to the neighbouring fence. "Your mum has to choose where to put her focus, doesn't she? She's probably waiting to confront her sister after this curse business is done."

A thump drew my attention to the bird feeder, where Tansy had successfully batted away a pigeon with her paws.

"She thinks *my* focus should be on removing slugs from people's gardens and not on the demons." I shook my head. "Also, Tansy has a new nemesis."

I told her about the other squirrel and its surprise owner, as well as my suspicions that both had been nosing around the town before the flower club leader's death.

"I bet this Nasturtium and her squirrel killed Araminta," said Piper. "And she gave you the fake list to lure you into a false sense of security."

"She might have." The thought had certainly crossed my

mind. "That doesn't mean she'll admit to anything. I've no idea what her squirrel's up to, either."

"Another red squirrel. No wonder Tansy's hopping mad." She tensed. "Ah, your mother's back. You'd better stop telling me your coven's secrets."

Sure enough, Mum had reappeared, no longer holding the list. "Robin, we need to make a plan."

"I thought this was the plan." I gestured to the garden. "That and finding a curse-breaker. Otherwise, isn't it up to Ramsey to question everyone who's on the list until someone admits to murdering Araminta?"

"Yes," she said. "However, my mother said Araminta's ghost would appear within the next day."

"Right. She did say that." She'd also insinuated that she would come to tell me in person if she showed up in the middle of the night, which I'd drawn the line at. "Grandma's a special case, and not everyone lingers after death."

"There's another way to ensure her appearance."

"What… summon her?" My heart began to beat faster. "I thought… I mean, I thought the afterworld was off-limits."

"Yes, this is a very dangerous time to summon anyone from the afterworld."

I thought of the demons and shivered. "It's possible to take precautions, like using sage…"

"I have an easier way," she said. "I intend to visit the Reaper myself tomorrow and ask for his help."

"He still hasn't answered his messages?" She must be getting desperate if she wanted to pay him a visit in person. "Okay, then we'll talk to him ourselves."

Mum said nothing, which set alarm bells ringing in my skull. "I'm going with you, right?"

"It's too—"

"Dangerous?" Disbelief bled into my voice. "Surely, the safest place from demons is right next to a Reaper."

"We can't both leave town at once," she said. "Given the circumstances, it's best for you to get on with your job as Head Witch."

My hands fisted. "This isn't going to make Aunt Shannon think I'm any more competent."

"She doesn't have to know."

"You don't think she won't spy on you again at the first opportunity?" Anger and frustration underlaid my tone. "She might do worse than set those slugs loose again if she knows you're away from the office, running errands on my behalf."

"There's no other way." She moved back towards the house. "Sorry, Robin."

*Sorry.* She never apologised to me. Hearing the word from her surprised me enough that some of my frustration momentarily disappeared. Some but not all.

I heaved a sigh. "We might not need the Reaper if we get lucky and Araminta's ghost shows up of her own accord."

I'd be better off waiting than risking my own neck, but if I couldn't talk to the Reaper myself, how was I supposed to fulfil the sceptre's mission?

8

Araminta's ghost did not show up overnight. Mercifully, neither did Grandma. As little as I'd wanted to be woken by her ghostly figure during the night, though, her absence spelled the end of any chances I might have had of Mum changing her mind on taking me to meet the local Reaper. At breakfast, she repeated the same arguments as the previous day between bouts of pacing around, walking in and out of the garden to check for intruders, and generally making me twitchy.

When Mum finally left, Ramsey watched her with a crease between his brows. "I wish she didn't have to go alone."

"She doesn't." I picked at my breakfast. "She insisted on leaving me behind. Anyway, you don't think Mum can handle herself?"

"I think there's a chance someone will lay a trap outside of Wildwood Heath," he replied. "The demons know you'll be planning to speak to the Reaper."

I shook my head. "If anything, that's an argument for me going with her. If she gets possessed, and she's alone…"

The thought made shivers spring to my arms, but Mum would have already cast a transportation spell and vanished by now. It was too late to follow her, and I didn't know where the Reaper lived.

*Why couldn't she just trust me?* The thought remained foremost in my mind as I walked to the office. Even Tansy was quieter than usual, though she declared that she'd patrol outside my office to make sure Aunt Shannon's familiar didn't try eavesdropping on any more sensitive conversations.

With Chloe filling in for Mum, I had only the company of sleeping Carmilla the cat to keep me on task, and I found myself waiting for my grandmother to show up for possibly the first time ever. I assumed she'd have let me know if Araminta's ghost had appeared overnight, but I had no focus for anything else. When Grandma did show up, I'd been watching my laptop screensaver of gambolling Eevees for twenty minutes.

"You look gloomy," she commented.

"It turns out Araminta was murdered," I said without preamble, "and she unleashed the curse herself."

"Excellent."

"What?" How did she manage to baffle me with her every reaction? "Does it not... bother you that your friend was murdered?"

"Oh, I guessed from the start," she said in cheery tones. "She can join the club."

"Grandma, do you *want* mum's rosebushes to be eaten by slugs? There are quite enough of them here at headquarters already."

"I know. I very much enjoyed watching you all recapture them yesterday."

"Thanks for that." So much for the revelation of Araminta's murder prompting her into action. "Clearly, this isn't a problem that's going to go away on its own. Have you seen Araminta's ghost yet?"

"Not yet, no," she said. "She must be hiding in the afterworld."

"That or she's moved on."

"No, she hasn't." Her jovial tone vanished, to be replaced with a warning note that indicated she'd start throwing papers around if I didn't take back my words.

"There's one way to find out where she is," I said hastily. "Summon her. But for obvious reasons, that's a terrible plan."

"I think it's an excellent idea," she said. "Go on, then."

"Do I need to remind you that there are a pair of demons who want me dead?" Yes, I did, apparently. "Mum's out of the office visiting a Reaper—"

I'd spoken without thinking, and Grandma cut in with a shrill cry. "A *Reaper?*"

A gust of wind arose, lifting papers into the air. Carmilla shrieked as the noise woke her up, while my coffee mug upended itself over the desk.

"Calm down!" I told her. "The Reaper's not coming to banish you. He's going to help me deal with *your* demons."

"Reaper!" She shrieked, the sound echoing, and all the cabinets rattled in agreement. A growing tornado swept up every paper in the room, and Carmilla shot out of the office like a bullet.

I followed fast on her heels and closed the door. Standing with my back to it, I caught my breath and winced when the door thumped against its frame. *I definitely should have gone with Mum instead.*

Chloe came running out of Mum's office. "Oh no."

"I made the mistake of mentioning the word 'Reaper,'" I whispered to her, grimacing as the door thumped in its frame again. "And insinuating that Araminta moved on."

"She'll calm down," said Chloe. "You know how sensitive she is."

"When Mum trusted me to handle things here on my own, I doubt she wanted me to get driven out of my own office by a ghost," I said ruefully. "Sorry. I should have thought before I spoke."

"It's all right," Chloe said. "You can come into your mother's office. There's plenty of space."

"I left my laptop behind." Not that I was keen to go back into Grandma's madhouse. With her screams ringing in my ears, I walked the short distance to Mum's office door. "And my paperwork."

"No problem." She lifted her wand again and conjured up my laptop and a pile of coffee-soaked papers, which landed on the desk. Mum's desk, which was as pristine as the rest of her office.

"As if Aunt Shannon needs another reason to believe I'm incompetent." I sank into a seat and rubbed my temples. "Did you know she stayed behind at the office yesterday to set the slugs loose in the garden?"

"Your mother told me." Her mouth turned down at the corners. "She also mentioned she was going to visit the Reaper…"

"Without me." I tried to keep the hurt out of my voice and failed. "I wish Araminta *had* shown up in the afterworld. Then I'd have something useful to do."

As a bonus, Grandma might stop screaming the place down if her friend showed up. Of course, I *could* try a summoning spell if I was willing to risk the demons answering my call. Even within the safety of a circle of sage, the risk was always present.

Or was it? One of the demons was currently possessing Leona, as far as I knew, while the other had been banished deeper into the afterworld courtesy of Maura. I didn't know the intricacies of all the laws governing the other side, but ghosts were far easier to summon than any other being that inhabited the nebulous state between life and true death. They didn't live in the same place that demons and other beasts did. There were doors in the way, keeping the monsters from getting out.

Chloe pursed her lips. "Robin, what are you thinking?"

"I'm thinking that it might shut her up if we summon Araminta's ghost," I replied. "If I set out a circle of sage and take all the necessary precautions, the worst that can happen is that she doesn't answer."

"I don't know." Chloe winced when Grandma gave another ear-splitting shriek. "Your mother wouldn't like it."

"She didn't explicitly give you instructions not to summon any ghosts, did she?" It wouldn't be the first time I'd summoned a ghost in the office, though admittedly, the last time had ended in Grandma rampaging around the place.

"No, but the afterworld..." Chloe shuddered. "It's dangerous."

"I know, but imagine if Mum invites the Reaper here and finds Grandma raising hell," I said. "He might banish her out of sheer annoyance."

It was a weak argument—Mum wouldn't bring the Reaper to headquarters unless another demon possessed someone—but Chloe's shoulders slumped. "If you're sure, there are supplies for summoning spells in the storeroom."

"I'll get them." I'd cast the spell before and knew how it worked, though a voice in the back of my head whispered that I was playing into the demons' hands by touching the afterworld at all.

*I have to do something,* I told myself. Speaking to Araminta would help us get to the bottom of both her murder and the curse she'd unleashed upon her death. Or I hoped it would.

I left Mum's office for the storeroom, where I selected the

right herbs from the shelves and carried them back to the office.

"I don't think Mum would want me summoning ghosts in here," I remarked to Chloe. "Is there a spare room we can use?"

"Sure." Chloe rose to her feet and led the way to a room a few doors down, which contained little except for a few tables and chairs. "I'll... I'll keep watch."

A guilty pang struck me for making her nervous, but the sound of Grandma's shrieking in the background doubled my resolve to quieten her down by any means possible. I helped Chloe move the tables and chairs against the walls of the room and then assembled the ingredients I'd gathered from the storeroom. I double-checked there were no gaps in the circle of sage in case the ghost decided to escape and join Grandma in wreaking havoc.

Speaking of whom... I figured she'd want to know what I was up to. I returned to my office and warily nudged the door open. Inside, Grandma had levitated every piece of furniture in the room and was alternating between wailing and screeching.

"Grandma," I said loudly. "I am going to summon Araminta. Do you still want to talk to her?"

"Araminta?" She stopped midshriek. "Is she here?"

"She will be." *I hope.* "But she won't want to stick around if you're screaming the place down."

"No need to be rude," she said. "Where is she?"

"I'm going to summon her into a spare room," I told her. "You can come in when you've calmed down."

I closed the door and returned to the spare room, while Chloe hovered in the background, fidgeting. I checked the circle of sage yet again, trying to convince myself that the most likely outcome was that I wouldn't find Araminta at all. It would be entirely typical if she'd gone off to the afterworld and left us to deal with all the nonsense she'd left behind.

*Here goes nothing.* I faced the circle and spoke in a clear voice. "I summon you, Araminta."

At first, nothing happened, and then, darkness began to rise within the circle like smoke from a fire. My heart gave a leap when a transparent figure appeared amid the darkness. While she was a tad more faded than she'd been the last time I'd seen her, Araminta wore the same unpleasant expression as she had when she was alive.

Then, she pointed at me and cackled. "Oh, Head Witch. I am *delighted* to see you."

"You cursed us." All my nerves fled, to be replaced by anger. "Thanks a bunch."

"Cursed you?" She laughed again. "I would never."

"We know you did." I glared at her. "We also know you were murdered."

"I knew it!" She spun on the spot, causing the chairs stacked against the wall to rattle. "I *knew* they'd bump me off eventually."

"Who?" I asked. "The flower club members?"

"Obviously."

"Anyone in particular?"

"I don't know. I'm a ghost, not psychic." She laughed loudly. "Now, where's your grandmother?"

"Grandma." I swivelled to the door, which had swung closed in the gust of wind stirred up by the ghost's arrival. "Grandma, did you want to talk to your friend?"

My grandmother didn't answer, but Chloe backed towards the door. "I'll find her."

Araminta drifted to the circle's edge and made a hissing noise. "She's not going to want to come near all this sage, is she? Horrible stuff."

"It's a precaution." *Dammit, Grandma. Where'd she gone?*

Granted, there was no guarantee my grandmother wouldn't make Araminta *less* cooperative, but now, I was alone with a ghost who had no reason to listen to a word I said. "Listen, if you want us to find out who killed you, you're going to have to give us some direction."

"I'm not going to have to do anything," she retaliated. "You don't give me orders anymore, *Head Witch*."

*That's how it's going to be, is it?* "I think you should know my Reaper friend is in town, and she's more than happy to banish you to the deeper afterworld permanently if you decide not to answer our questions."

Her expression changed to alarm. "You're lying."

"I'm not. The Reaper is called Maura." I pulled out my phone. "She can be here in two seconds if I call her."

"Fine!" she yelped. "I'll tell you what you want to know."

"The curse," I said. "How'd you do it?"

"I didn't."

My heart missed a beat. "You didn't curse anyone?"

"No," she said. "I couldn't figure out how to set up the curse to come into effect after I died. That kind of magic isn't my strong point."

"It isn't?" Crap. That was a wrench I hadn't seen coming. Unless she was lying, but she seemed scared enough of the prospect of a Reaper showing up to have completely dropped her usual arrogance. "Then where did the slugs come from?"

"That's the question, isn't it?"

A moment of silence followed. *If she's right... who did set up the curse?* It didn't necessarily mean the same person had killed Araminta, either.

"You really don't know who killed you?" I asked. "Did you invite anyone into your house the day you died?"

"No," she said, "but I did host a flower club meeting the previous night."

"I thought you didn't want the others going anywhere near your plants."

"Now the flower contest is over, I'm an open and generous host." Her face fell. "Or I *was*. What kind of awful person would break the rules of hospitality in such a way?"

"Erm…" I thought back to my last encounter with Araminta's daughter. "Who's mentioned in your will, out of curiosity?"

Behind me, the door creaked inwards, and Chloe re-entered the spare room. "Sorry… your grandmother said she won't go near the sage."

"What does she want me to do? I'm not getting rid of it." Not when the sage barrier was the one defence between me and the afterworld.

"Why not?" Araminta drifted up to the circle's edge again, craning her neck to peer behind Chloe. "Your grandmother should be allowed to go wherever she likes. Ghosts have rights, too, you know."

"Technically, you don't." Fine. I'd do this myself. "Never mind my grandmother. Who was meant to inherit your belongings after you died? Your daughter?"

"*Her?*" She spoke in a sharp tone that rattled the chairs on the wall and caused one of them to fall over at the edge of the circle of sage.

*Oh no.* I ran around the room to check if the circle had broken, but it didn't look like it had. "Can you not do that?"

"Why?" A wicked grin appeared on her face. "Do you think I'm dangerous?"

"No, but there are other things in the afterworld that I don't want in here."

Araminta laughed, and a gust of wind swept outwards from the circle and knocked several more chairs over. This time, they landed *in* the circle, straight on top of the sage barrier.

"Hey!" I ran to pick up the chairs. "Stop that."

She gave a loud cackle, and to my alarm, darkness began to seep out of the circle and across the room.

"That's not supposed to happen." I jerked backwards, my heart plunging. "Go away. Araminta, I'm banishing you back into the afterworld."

She didn't move, but a patch of darkness appeared behind her, forming the outline of a figure. Maybe it was a trick of the light, but the shape seemed... almost solid. *What—?*

"Hey!" I raised the sceptre, panic blaring in my mind. "I'll call the Reaper. I'm warning you."

"It's not me!" Fear flickered in the ghost's eyes. "Help!"

She extended a hand over the circle's edge, grabbing my wrist and tugging hard. The sensation was solid, sharp, cold.

Then everything went black.

———

I stood in utter darkness. Or rather, drifted. I couldn't feel my body, and to be honest, I wasn't sure my body was even here. Nothing but utter blackness clouded my vision, engulfing all my senses.

And as I drifted, I heard a quiet, feminine voice. "This isn't how I expected to meet you."

I squinted into the pitch-blackness that smothered the world, feeling a chill of familiarity. This intense darkness could only be the deeper afterworld, the same place I'd seen when Maura had banished the demons, and the disembodied voice... Who was it?

"I can't be dead!" I gasped out. At least I had a voice, though I didn't feel my mouth move when I spoke.

"You aren't," said the voice. "But you're closer to death than any living person ought to be."

"Who are you?" Questions crash-landed in my head. "What happened?"

"You walked into a trap intended to kill you." A shadowy figure appeared, dark even against the absolute blackness. "In fact, it should have succeeded."

"You're the Reaper." Fear washed over me. "Have you come to take my soul?"

"Not yet."

"Then what's… I mean, what's happening to me?" I gestured at my surroundings and glimpsed a faint outline in the shape of my hand. Like a ghost. *No. No, please, no.*

"You touched the afterworld," she said. "You summoned the dead."

"In a circle of sage." Or I had until that pesky ghost had decided to drag me into the—into the realm of the dead. *How, though?*

The Reaper tutted. "Sage isn't enough when you're dealing with a creature that strong. The ghost was a pawn, sent by the demons, to drag you into the afterworld."

"Araminta was sent by the demons?" Had that been what I'd seen behind her? "If I'm in the afterworld, doesn't that mean I'm dead by definition?"

If I perished, what would happen to my family? Would the demon go after them? Or would that honour go to the unlucky soul who claimed the sceptre next?

Would the sceptre claim anyone at all?

*No. I can't be dying.* If I was, I'd lose any chance of escaping the role of Head Witch. I'd never get to achieve anything on my own terms. Harvey and I would never get to—

"Luckily, you found me." The Reaper's ghostly form moved closer. "We Reapers have certain… skills. I'm not, strictly speaking, supposed to use them in this manner, but what my mentor doesn't know won't hurt him."

"Mentor?" Wait. "Was that the Reaper Mum went to meet with?"

"Yes," she said. "I'm Linnea, his apprentice. Don't worry, I'm trained enough for this."

That didn't sound entirely reassuring, but I was half dead, a transparent floating figure in a void of darkness. I didn't exactly have a lot of choice in the matter.

"Don't panic." She looked me in the eyes, or I thought so. Being a shadow, it was hard to tell. "This is going to be painful."

"Wait," I said. "What do you mean by that?"

Instead of answering, she held out a hand formed entirely of shadow. When I extended my own hand to take hers, her grip solidified, and the darkness faded away.

## 9

When I opened my eyes, I found myself in my own bedroom. How had I got there? More to the point, why were Mum and Ramsey sitting beside my bed as though… as though I was dying? Crap. My body felt stiff, unsteady. Jerkily, I lifted a hand to my face and brushed against a soft, fluffy tail.

Tansy jumped upright with a screech. "You're alive!"

"I am." My voice felt rusty, unused. "What happened?"

"You did something incredibly dangerous, Robin," Mum told me.

"I did?" My memories trickled back in. "Weren't you talking to the—?"

Reaper. I'd spoken to her myself. She'd saved my life.

I pushed upright into a sitting position, my head throbbing with pain as if it'd been used for drum practise. My body felt like a wrung-out sponge.

"Lie back down," Mum said sharply. "You don't want to overexert yourself."

"No, I want to find Araminta's ghost and strangle her," I replied. "And then do the same to Grandma."

"Oh, my mother is in the doghouse, don't worry." A chilling note underlaid her voice. "Chloe told me what she did to your office."

"That and she left me to interrogate her delightful friend alone." My hands clenched into fists. "Also, Araminta claimed she never cursed anyone at all."

"I don't care about Araminta," Mum said tersely. "That's Ramsey's job."

Ramsey just stared at me, his face as white as a sheet.

"Arrested anyone yet?" I attempted a breezy tone, but my annoyance at Araminta was somewhat dampened by my brush with death. More than a brush—I'd gone swimming in the afterworld—yet here I was. Alive and angry.

Ramsey narrowed his eyes. "Go back to sleep."

I made a noise of protest, but just talking had exhausted me, and Tansy climbed onto my chest and pushed me downwards.

"Hey," I muttered feebly. "I'm okay."

I was already halfway to passing out before I'd finished speaking, and when my eyes next opened, it was to the improbable sight of Harvey sitting in a chair next to the bed.

Harvey. In my room. In my mother's house. I blinked, but Harvey didn't disappear.

"Am I dreaming?" I croaked.

"If you are, so am I." Harvey leaned over and carefully hugged me. "Robin, you scared the hell out of me."

"Wasn't deliberate." I hugged him back then collapsed onto the pillow. "How long have you been here?"

"Not long," he replied. "I called your phone so many times your family got fed up and let me in."

Whoa. "Wait, what day is it?"

"Sunday."

Crap. Pushing the covers back, I sat up. "Mum will have piled all the work I missed onto my desk, I'm sure."

"Robin." Mum herself materialised in the doorway, her suspicious gaze darting between me and Harvey.

"Yes?" I was not in the mood for a fight, with my body still feeling as though I'd had a fight with a wall and lost. "I'm getting up."

"Get back into bed," Mum ordered.

"I'm still *in* bed, technically," I protested. "Also, I want to know what I missed at the office. Let me guess, Aunt Shannon has managed to make this my fault?"

"I don't care what my sister thinks," she said. "And I won't discuss the rest in front of non-coven members."

She looked at Harvey, who ducked his head. "Sorry, I'll wait outside."

I glared at my mother as he slipped out of the room. "There's no need to be rude to him. He cares about me. A lot."

"I'm aware," she said testily, "but you wanted to discuss the coven, and things at the office are somewhat... heated."

"Why, because of the slugs?" I'd almost forgotten our slimy little problem. "Or because the others found out about me summoning ghosts on the property?"

"Very luckily, my mother was willing to take credit for causing all the chaos herself," she said. "Which makes explaining your predicament trickier. I told the rest of the witches that you were attacked by demons, which is more or less the truth."

"Great." I slumped against the pillow again. "Wait. Has Aunt Shannon told everyone about my mission? She hasn't, has she?"

"No," she said, "but she's made it quite clear what she thinks of your ability to handle the demons, and to be honest, she's not wrong."

Her words stung like a swarm of wasps, battering my already bruised body. "You... You don't think I can handle them? Isn't this exactly what you've been preparing me for?"

"Not to summon ghosts into the coven headquarters and nearly get yourself killed." Her tone was sharp, and while a rational part of me knew her anger was a cover for genuine fear, her lack of faith in me burned all the same.

"I told you, it wasn't my idea," I said in brittle tones. "It was perfectly safe before Araminta decided to knock the sage over and release a demon into the spare room."

"There's always a risk with ghosts." She pinched the bridge of her nose between her fingertips. "The Reaper's apprentice told me as much. It turns out he's out of town on a mission, which is why he wasn't answering his calls, and it's incredibly lucky that Linnea found you before you got yourself killed."

My mouth parted. *I spoke to her.* The words were on my tongue, but I was too tired, too worn down to open that line of conversation right now. Especially with Harvey right outside the door.

On wobbly legs, I pushed to my feet. "I'm going to shower. Don't look at me like that. I want to see somewhere that isn't my room."

Mum watched like a statue with her hands clenched at her sides as I walked past her and out of the room, where I found Harvey hovering awkwardly in the hallway.

"Sorry," he said. "I'll go…"

"You don't have to, but it's not going to be much fun around here for a while." I gave a meaningful look at my mother's statue-like figure behind the door. "First, I'll see if I can get through a shower without passing out."

"Don't overdo it." He gave me a smile. "Text me? If you're awake?"

"Of course." As much as I wanted to hug him, I hadn't showered in days, and my hair was in dire need of a wash. "See you soon."

I did indeed manage to get through the shower without

passing out, and then I changed into a clean T-shirt and a pair of jogging trousers. Expecting to walk downstairs might have been a bit too optimistic, but I held onto the wall for balance and had almost made it to the foot of the stairs when I spied Ramsey standing in the hallway, his back to the wall.

I staggered down the last few steps. "What are you doing lurking around here?"

He shrugged, his eyes underscored with shadows. Had he even slept since I'd been attacked? "You shouldn't be walking."

"You need a nap," I retaliated.

Mum stuck her head out of the living room. "Robin, you aren't well enough to walk."

"I am fine. Check on your other child." I jabbed a finger in Ramsey's general direction. "I'm starving."

"Kimberly will cook you a meal. If you must stay downstairs, sit *down*."

"Fine, fine." I entered the living room and found the sofa mostly occupied by cats. Horace, Mum's familiar, lay beside Carmilla, who eyed me with mild interest.

"Oh, you are alive," she remarked. "I thought your mother was in denial."

"Thanks for that. And you can thank your witch for my ending up in this state to begin with."

She coughed up a hairball in response. I sidestepped her and flopped into an armchair, lacking the energy to verbally spar with Grandma's familiar.

Ramsey came into the room and turned on the TV. He then sat in the other armchair without speaking a word.

"Hey." I craned my neck to watch him. "You're not at work?"

"No, I took the day off."

My mouth fell open. "You did *what*?"

He hadn't voluntarily taken a day off in years, I was sure. I was pretty sure he'd show up at work if he was dead. That hadn't stopped Grandma, after all.

He ignored my question. "You can pick the movie."

I was tempted to make a joke about him being possessed by a demon, but that would have been too soon. Instead, I picked out the extended editions of *The Lord of the Rings*, figuring that I might as well make the most of our temporary truce, and banished all thoughts of demons and Reapers from my mind.

For now.

———

I'd expected Mum to want to haul me into the office the following morning, but I was instead greeted at breakfast by a mountain of paperwork stacked on the kitchen table next to the cereal.

"Mum… what is this?" I asked when she walked into the kitchen, carrying yet another stack of papers.

She put down her burden on the already crammed table. "You still aren't well enough to come back into the office, but I thought you could start catching up on what you missed. If you're up for it."

"I don't think I am." I faked a cough, like I was a teenager trying to convince my parents to let me skip school. "Please tell me you aren't bringing the council here to host meetings in the living room as well."

"Of course not," she said. "There are a limited number of people allowed into the house."

"Good." I moved a stack of papers aside so I could reach my plate. "What on earth is urgent enough that it needs doing right this second? More condolence letters?"

"No," she said shortly. "Chloe will be along soon to help you out."

I pointedly ignored the stacks of paperwork while I ate breakfast and watched Tansy run amok in the back garden. I still hadn't addressed the elephant in the room—or rather, the Reaper-shaped shadow hovering over my shoulder—and while I hadn't wanted to break the fragile peace between us, I'd rather do almost anything than look at paperwork.

When I'd finished eating, I decided to take the plunge. "You mentioned contacting the Reaper's apprentice when you went to find him?"

"Yes," Mum answered. "I told her that you'd come and see her as soon as you were well."

"Oh." I fidgeted. "I might have already spoken to her. In the afterworld."

Mum spun to me, her eyes widening. "You spoke to the Reaper?"

"She's the one who saved my neck." I ploughed on before she could interrupt. "She told me the demons somehow tricked Araminta into trying to drag me into the afterworld and get me killed. If she hadn't been there, I wouldn't have been able to get out."

The colour drained from Mum's face. "Then it's even more important that we speak to her again as soon as possible."

"I thought I was supposed to be dealing with this." I gestured to the table. "Now do you see why I think handling paperwork is a waste of time?"

"Chloe will handle most of it," she said. "I'll call the Reaper."

She'd changed her tune fast. "Should I contact Maura too?"

"She's not an official Reaper," said Mum. "It's unlikely that she'll be able to do anything that the local Reaper's apprentice can't do better."

Hmm. "If you say so. Wait—is Araminta's ghost still around? I didn't banish her."

Mum's eyes narrowed. "I never asked, but she certainly hasn't shown herself to anyone at the office."

I pushed to my feet. I still felt a bit shaky, but I was done with lying in bed. "I'm going to look for her."

"You most certainly aren't," she said. "You aren't even going to speak to my mother, not until the Reaper has confirmed that there are no more traps in the afterworld."

"Did you tell Grandma?" My thoughts went back to the chaos she'd caused in my office. She must know her antics had, in part, caused my brush with death, but in her current erratic state, it was anyone's guess as to whether she'd experience any sense of regret.

Tansy came scampering into the house from the back garden, chewing on something that sounded suspiciously like a sunflower seed, and jumped onto the table. "What's all this?"

"Work." I pulled a face. "Apparently, I'm back at the office. Or the office has come to me. Is everything okay outside?"

"No squirrels, red or otherwise," she said. "I patrolled the whole forest."

"You did." A thought jolted me. "Mum… have you told Dad?"

A moment passed. "Ramsey did."

Better than nobody telling him at all. "Did he come to the house? He must have. Why'd you let Harvey in and not him?"

Mum didn't look abashed in the least. "He said some unkind things to me."

That didn't sound like Dad. Heart thumping, I went to fetch my shoes. "I'm going to see him." When Mum opened her mouth to protest, I added, "Don't you start. I can't just leave him not knowing if I'm alive."

I pulled on my shoes shakily while Tansy came hurrying over. "I can go instead."

"He can't understand you, Tansy." I reached out and stroked her. "I'll be fine. We'll go together."

I marched out of the door, pushing aside my fatigue and shakiness, while Tansy ran ahead of me. I had to stop and rest a couple of times on the forest path, but when I reached the cottage, Dad already waited outside with Tansy bouncing up and down at his feet. Pale-faced, he strode forwards and hugged me. "Robin… I'm so glad you're okay."

"I can't believe Mum didn't let you into the house." I hugged him back. "What did you say to her?"

He released me, his mouth curving in a frown. "I may have lost my temper with her."

"You, lose your temper? Really?"

"I couldn't stand it," he murmured. "Her devotion to this Head Witch ridiculousness has been putting you in danger from the start, but this… I thought we lost you."

His vehemence surprised me. "I mean, technically, it was the ghost of one of Grandma's friends who nearly got me killed. Not being Head Witch."

"That's no better, Robin."

"I know." My eyes stung with tears. "I'm sorry I worried you. I'm also sorry Mum was… Mum."

"Your brother came to see me right away and told me you were alive," he said. "I was glad of that, at least."

"Yeah." I hugged him again, trying not to cry. "It won't happen again."

"I wish…" He faltered. "I can't do anything to help you. That's the worst part."

"Robin." Ramsey came jogging into view from behind me. "You shouldn't be here alone."

"Clearly, I'm not alone." I gestured to Dad and to Tansy, who hopped onto a low-hanging branch and wagged her tail threateningly at my brother. "I told Mum I'd be fine. We're surrounded by sage here. No ghosts are going to start throwing tantrums, don't worry."

"That's not the point." Ramsey flushed. "Come on. Let's go."

I might have argued the point, but my energy levels were flagging more than I wanted to admit. "Dad, I'll see you soon?"

"Of course." He hugged me one last time before Ramsey steered me away, his hand on my shoulder.

I tugged myself free. "This is ridiculous. I can walk, you know."

"You should still be resting." He scowled when Tansy hopped onto a branch above, causing leaves to shower down onto his head. "You went through an ordeal."

"I'm not the only one." I gestured behind me as Dad closed the cottage door. "This Head Witch crap doesn't only affect our immediate family. Also, shouldn't you be at the office? I thought you were looking for Araminta's killer."

"I have been," he said. "I questioned every flower club member over the course of two days, and frankly, they're all equally likely to have killed her. None confessed."

"What about her daughter?"

"She has an alibi," he replied. "Backed up by several people I called."

"That squirrel of hers, though." I glanced up at Tansy, who'd overtaken us in her quest to chase off a blackbird. "He was in town the same day that Araminta died."

His jaw twitched in annoyance. "Unfortunately, he seems to have disappeared."

"He has?" I queried. "Isn't he with Nasturtium?"

"He didn't show up when I questioned her," he said. "She tried to deny everything, but if we're to believe Araminta didn't enact the curse herself, her daughter is the most likely person to have been responsible."

"Why not ask her to undo it, then?"

"It's not that simple." Frustration underlaid his tone. "Just *asking* her to undo the curse isn't enough, not when she denies all responsibility."

"I could ask Maura to pay her a visit."

"Robin."

"Joking, joking." I had to admit it was tempting, though, especially given her mother's antics in the afterworld. Besides, I'd had about enough of being coddled.

When I found Mum waiting outside the house with yet another stack of paperwork in her arms, my temper frayed even further.

"Enough." I jabbed my finger towards the coven head-quarters. "Take those papers back to my office. Take the rest too."

"There's no need to shout."

"There's no need to act as if I'm on my deathbed." A flutter of wings from the neighbouring fence warned me that Aunt Shannon's familiar was listening out for the latest drama, which further incensed me. "I'm either going back to work or to bed, and I'm done with the latter."

No. I'd survived, and I'd make sure that everyone knew it. Including the demons.

10

To my utmost surprise, Mum caved in and let me go back to work that afternoon. It probably said something about my level of boredom that I was more relieved to finally have a change of scenery than anything else.

Chloe greeted me like I was a dead woman walking when I entered the office. "I'm glad you made it, Robin. I'm sorry I couldn't help you."

"It's not your fault." I wouldn't have her blaming herself for this, not when there was quite enough blame to go around already. "I'm fine now. Have you seen Grandma?"

"No, I… haven't been here in the last few days." She sank back into her seat.

She might as well have said she'd been to the moon. "What on earth have you been doing, then?"

Chloe dropped her gaze to the mountain of paperwork Mum had generously returned to the office. "Helping your mother."

*What's she up to this time?* Annoyance prickled at me. Hadn't she learned from the recent incident that leaving me out of her plans was no guarantee I wouldn't run into demon-related trouble? "Have you seen Aunt Shannon? Her familiar was spying on the house, so I'm guessing she's been as much of a nightmare as ever."

"Terrible." Her hands clenched, her knuckles whitening. "Even worse than usual."

"What, gloating?"

"No, she was dropping false apologies and pretending to be sorry." She shuddered. "That's more horrifying."

"I'm glad I slept through that," I commented. "No coven meeting today?"

"No, but there's one tomorrow unless we reschedule."

"I bet Aunt Shannon would love another excuse to label me as incompetent." I released a sigh. "Even Mum said I'm not ready to face the demons. I'm guessing that's why she has you running errands."

She flinched. "It's not... I'm not trying to keep things from you."

"I know. It's Mum's fault." She didn't deserve to be yelled at, but I'd about had it with my family's attempts to wrap me in cotton wool. "Are the slugs still in the coven's maze? Any new incidents?"

"I think so," she mumbled. "I didn't hear of anyone else getting hit by the curse."

Her lack of certainty was unusual. I might have had the temptation to make a joke about demonic possession, but nobody would appreciate that, and besides, I had a bone to pick with the office's other inhabitant.

"Grandma," I called out to the back corner of the room. "I know you're in here."

"She hasn't been answering," Chloe said.

"Maybe she will when Mum calls the Reaper back."

"No, she won't." Grandma appeared behind my desk

without so much as an expression of remorse on her face. "I'm not having any more Reapers in my home."

"You should have thought of that before you let your ghostly friend run around making trouble," I retaliated. "She nearly killed me."

"Araminta didn't do anything wrong," she said. "It's not her fault that nasty demon ambushed her."

"It wasn't the demon who knocked a bunch of chairs into the sage circle." I folded my arms across my chest. "As for you, if you hadn't thrown a tantrum, I wouldn't have been left to interrogate your friend alone."

"Enough cheek from you," she said. "I'm the Head Witch. Did you forget?"

"You haven't been Head Witch in months," I said through gritted teeth. "And we nearly had *no* Head Witch when I almost got killed. How would you have felt about that?"

"Death isn't so bad," she said pensively. "It'd be a shame, but I think we could make it fun."

Okay, she was officially out of her mind. "Grandma, if I die, who's going to deal with those demons? The ones the sceptre chose *me* to get rid of in your place?"

"Oh, don't be such a worrywart. That's your mother's job." She waved a hand, rustling the papers on the desk. "I'm sure the sceptre will pick someone else."

"I'd still be *dead*." Which might not mean that much to someone who'd been outside of the land of the living for months now, but it mattered a lot to me, thanks. And it rankled that one of my first thoughts when I'd been on the brink of death had been that I hadn't fulfilled my mission yet and my family didn't think of me as worthy. Yes, my mother would probably be the better choice. I *knew* that, yet I felt a pang of annoyance at myself for being drawn into the façade of being Head Witch despite the absolute lack of gratitude from most people in my life.

"That's enough sulking from you." Grandma swatted me with a transparent hand. "You *nearly* died. I'm the one who up and finished the job."

"Because someone murdered you." I glared at her. "If you're fishing for sympathy, it's not going to work. You just implied that it didn't matter if I died."

"Don't twist my words, Robin Wildwood," she said. "I was trying to assuage your hand-wringing over the sceptre and this little mission you've taken upon yourself to fulfil."

"This little mission is to banish the demons *you* angered," I pointed out. "Don't act as if this is my choice."

Grandma gave an irritated huff. "None of us have a choice. I'm dead, you're alive, and you want to banish me altogether, don't you?"

"Now who's twisting words?" I shook my head at her. "Nobody's saying you can't stay here, but I'm Head Witch now. The office is mine, and if you trash the place, guess who gets blamed."

"You threatened me with sage," she said indignantly. "I know you think I'm less than a person, but you wouldn't threaten to cut off your brother's head if he moved your favourite Pokerman."

"Sage isn't the same as beheading someone. Also, it's Pokémon." In a convoluted way, maybe she had a point, though. "Look, I'm not going to have you banished, but you need to get over your irrational attitude towards Reapers if you want me to get rid of those demons."

"If you worked with genuine Reapers rather than *rogues*, I'd be more than happy to let them do as they wish," she said sourly. "The Reaper *I* worked with was respectful and kind."

"His apprentice saved my life," I told her. "Also—have you seen Araminta since then?"

"Poor Araminta." She sniffed. "No, I haven't."

"I have no sympathy for *her*, given that she almost got me

killed." I looked to Chloe, who was typing away, seemingly oblivious to the heated conversation taking place right next to her desk. "I figured she might have stuck around to find her killer. Or haunt her daughter."

"You are a cruel person." Grandma crossed the room in a dramatic glide. "I shall find Araminta and tell her exactly what you said to me."

"Go right ahead." I rested my head on my hand and then jumped when a scream rang out from the direction of the coven's garden. "What was that?"

Chloe leapt to her feet. "Not again."

"The slugs?" I guessed, rising from my seat and grabbing my sceptre. My legs and arms protested at the exertion, and though I tried not to move too quickly, I was out of breath by the time I reached the back doors.

As I'd suspected, slugs covered the entire lawn. A number of other witches watched from the patio behind the door, including a serene-looking Aunt Shannon.

"Oh, good, you're alive." Her words were about as genuine as a full set of false nails. "I was starting to wonder if my sister was hiding your body to avoid anyone else claiming that sceptre of yours."

I ignored the jab. "Is this what you've been doing all week? Setting slugs loose and making other people clean them up?"

The rest of the coven goggled at me, but my filter had officially jumped ship. Aunt Shannon offered me an expression of polite incredulity in return.

"Certainly not," she said. "*My* work is for the good of the coven, unlike some people's. Given how much you've complained constantly of the demands of being Head Witch, it's understandable that you'll have seized on the first available chance to take a little holiday."

"Almost dying is not a holiday." Since none of the others

seemed inclined to help, I lifted the sceptre. It seemed heavier than I remembered, and my first attempt to levitate the slugs was a dismal failure. Heat rose to my face at the smirk on Aunt Shannon's face, which widened when Mum came sprinting into view with her wand in hand.

As Mum began levitating the slugs back into the buckets, I adjusted my grip on the sceptre and managed to aim properly this time. Kind of. I couldn't quite levitate the slugs as far as the buckets, so I dropped them on the patio instead, which had the bonus of causing the other witches to run back into headquarters to avoid being covered in slime. Only Aunt Shannon remained in place, while I fought the urge to drop the bucket on her head and make it look like an accident.

"Are you going to do anything useful?" I shot at her between bouts of levitating slugs. "Why are you out here, exactly?"

"Is it so wrong that I care for the well-being of my fellow witches?"

"No, it's untrue." My magic responded to my annoyance, drawing every bird in the vicinity, and the feathers showering upon the garden did nothing to improve the general chaos. Finally, drenched in sweat and at the end of my tether, I stood back to let Mum finish with the slugs, while Aunt Shannon hovered behind me like an even less appealing Grim Reaper.

Mum waved her wand in a sharp movement, and the buckets shot across the garden to the maze. "Shannon, stop hassling my daughter."

"I'm doing nothing of the sort," she said blithely. "Enjoy the rest of your day."

As she vanished back into the building, I glared after her. "I know she did this."

Sudden exhaustion hit me, and when I swayed on the

spot, Mum peered at my face. "I knew it was too soon for you to come back to work."

"I was fine until someone decided to redecorate the lawn." I lowered my aching hands. "I'm out of practise, but I can still do my job."

"I don't think so," she said. "You can take the rest of the afternoon off."

"What good will that do?" I jerked my head in the direction of the coven headquarters. "You know I'd be proving her point."

"Better than falling asleep at your desk." She gave me a stern look. "You can start afresh tomorrow."

A flash of red fur above the fence heralded Tansy's arrival, and she scampered down to join me. "We can go and see Rowan. I already told her you were back at work."

"Thanks, Tansy." That reminded me—I had an unending list of people I needed to check in with who'd want to know I was all right after my trip over to the afterworld. To my mum, I added, "Fine, but I'm not going home."

I expected her to argue the point, but she simply sighed as if to say "your funeral" and then went back to work.

I, meanwhile, made for Were's My Coffee? Tansy rode on my shoulder, offering support whenever I had to stop to rest. I doubted Rowan had been on my mum's priority list of people to keep updated on my condition if she hadn't even let my dad into the house, so I could only imagine how worried she'd been.

When I entered the café, Rowan abandoned the drink she was making and ran straight up to me. "Robin, are you okay?"

"I'm all right," I insisted. "Sorry if Mum took a while to tell you."

"My *mother* is the one who told me." Disgust filled her

tone. "She walked in here and was practically smirking at you being on your deathbed."

"That's horrible." A rush of anger seized me. "Chloe said she was pretending to be sorry."

"That, too." Rowan hugged me hard, and Tansy wrapped her tail around both of our necks, while Ralph the tarantula poked a hairy leg out of Rowan's sleeve too. "It was awful. Please don't do that to us again."

"Believe me, I'm not planning on making a habit of wandering into the afterworld." I released her, conscious that the few patrons in the café were watching curiously. "I'll tell you more later, but your mum… She knows about the demons, too. I can only assume she's planning to use it against me when my guard is down. When she isn't setting the slugs loose, that is."

"That was *her*?"

"What—no, she's not the person who used the curse." I didn't *think* so, anyway. "But she keeps moving the buckets in the coven's garden and making me clean up after her. When does your shift end?"

"In an hour," she replied. "Ah, should you really be walking around? You look exhausted."

"Don't you start." I sighed. "I've barely been back at work an afternoon, and my mother is acting as though I tried to climb Everest. Can't one of you act normal?"

She took a step back. "Sorry, Robin."

My heart sank. "I didn't mean to snap at you. I know everyone was worried."

"Yeah." She bit her lower lip. "I should get back to work. See you in an hour?"

"If I'm awake." Like it or not, I *was* tired. "Sorry again."

I left, my cheeks burning with shame. While my body ached for rest, the police station was nearby, and I hadn't set foot in there since before my brush with death.

"I'm going to see how the murder investigation is going," I muttered to Tansy. "Then I'll appease Mum and go to bed. I wonder if Ramsey's arrested anyone yet."

"I hope he arrests that squirrel" was Tansy's reply. "I *still* haven't found him yet. Not for lack of trying."

"Weird."

When I entered the police station, Julian gawped at me as though I'd returned from the dead. "Robin?"

"That's me," I said breezily. "No, I'm not possessed."

"I have to check." He rose upright and threw a handful of sage into my face, causing me to stumble and grab the desk for balance.

Tansy jumped off my shoulder with a squeak. "Hey!"

"See? No demon could be this uncoordinated." I pushed away from the desk. "Is Ramsey in?"

Ramsey sprang up from behind a door as though I'd summoned him up with his name. "Robin, you shouldn't be here."

I picked sage out of my hair. "I'd like an update on the investigation into Araminta's death."

"There's nothing you can do here," he said. "I sent Araminta's daughter home after her initial arrest."

I hadn't known he'd arrested Nasturtium at all. "How long did you have her in here?"

"Three days," he said. "She denied any involvement in her mother's death."

"What, you kept her in the holding cells?" I held out a hand as Tansy came running back over, shaking bits of sage out of her fur. "Did you ask her about the curse? And the document being a fake?"

"She didn't confess to anything," he said. "The document being faked isn't a crime, unless it *is* cursed. I've been trying to get in touch with curse-breakers, but I believe our mother was forced to put that task aside after—"

"After my near-death experience, I know," I finished. "Also, Aunt Shannon set the slugs loose again. She's getting to be as much of a nuisance as the person who originally used the curse, and if Araminta's ghost doesn't show up again, we won't have anyone else to question."

Anger flared in his eyes. "If her ghost *does* show up, I'll handle her myself."

"Will you now?" I took a startled step back, and my legs protested, threatening to fold underneath me. Even though I'd left the sceptre behind, my whole body ached, and I could tell from the tightening in his jaw that my brother had noticed. "Fine, let me know if you have any updates."

I left the police station before he could do something extreme like carry me home in person. Tansy kept up a steady stream of encouragement as I walked step by painful step, fighting the urge to lie down and fall asleep there and then. When the house came into view, I used my last burst of energy to hurry to the front door.

My plan was to go straight up to my room, but the shadowy figure waiting on the other side of the door squashed that plan.

*The Reaper.*

11

I hadn't been mentally prepared to see the Reaper this soon, and the shock of her appearance temporarily washed away my tiredness. "Erm... hi. Does my mother know you're in her house?"

In person, Linnea was a little more solid than she'd been in the afterworld. And shorter. She was around my height, her pale face framed by a cloud of black hair that defied gravity in a way that a regular person could never achieve without a ton of hairspray. A modest black dress hugged her body to knee-length, and the faint shadow of the afterworld at her back completed the ensemble.

Mum came out of the living room. "There you are, Robin."

I swivelled to her. "I didn't know you were setting up the meeting today."

A tense moment passed during which her gaze darted between us. "Neither did I."

Uh-oh. If the Reaper had taken my mother by surprise, someone was getting a verbal skewering, and I had no intention of putting myself in the firing line. On the other hand, how many times would a Reaper pay me a visit in person?

"I thought, given the attempt on your daughter's life, that it would be unwise to delay," said Linnea. "My mentor is still out of town, so I stepped in."

"Is that normal?" I asked her. "Do Reapers often go on sabbatical?"

"They have occasional gatherings with the Reaper Council, which can take a few days or weeks," she said. "Luckily, before he left, he told me about your little demon problem."

"Oh. Good." I glanced at Mum, not sure how she wanted me to handle this. "He helped my grandmother banish the demons, right? Buried them deep enough in the afterworld that it's taken them twenty-odd years to escape?"

"Yes." She glided into the living room and claimed the sofa; the two cats who normally occupied the space were noticeably absent. "When demons fixate on a person... to be frank, there's not much you can do to escape their notice. They're immortal, after all, and banishing them deep into the afterworld is like tossing a sea serpent's egg into the deep ocean. Sooner or later, it'll surface again."

I couldn't say I was a fan of that analogy. Apparently, Tansy wasn't, either, because she took off for the back door like a hellbeast was on her tail.

Linnea watched with mild amusement. "Animals don't usually like me."

*I'm not surprised.* There was something *cold* about her presence, even though she was clothed in the appearance of a regular human. Fighting a shiver, I sat down in one of the armchairs. "Did your mentor tell you about Leona?"

She arched a thin brow. "Who?"

"A local witch who made a deal with one of the demons," Mum explained. "She's the current host—as far as we know and assuming she's still alive."

"I wouldn't bet on that," said the Reaper. "Making a deal with a demon is a swift ticket to the grave, make no mistake. However, if you know the person the demon is possessing, it'll be easier to find them."

"It wasn't her who tried to kill me the other day, though, was it?" I asked. "I mean—she isn't here in Wildwood Heath."

"A demon was responsible for the attack, certainly," said Linnea.

My blood chilled. "The demon was there? In the coven's headquarters?"

"No," she said, "but it had an influence on the ghost. When she touched you, you were pulled into the afterworld."

"I didn't know that was possible." As was abundantly clear, though, there was a world of knowledge off-limits to anyone except Reapers.

"Regardless," Mum interjected, "what we need to know is how to stop it from happening again. There are other ghosts present in town, including my own mother. How do we know the demons won't target her next?"

"If you keep the ghost contained within a circle of sage, that should be enough of a deterrent," Linnea replied.

"Grandma would love that," I muttered. "And we don't know if Araminta's ghost is still in the building as well."

"Was she the ghost that attacked you?" asked the Reaper. "I'd suggest you get rid of her as quickly as possible. I can help."

"That won't be necessary," Mum said. I was surprised she'd turn down the offer, but maybe she didn't want Linnea to take matters too far and banish Grandma as well. "However, if you can help us find the demon's current location, it would be appreciated."

"I didn't sense any demons in the immediate vicinity," said Linnea. "If I had to guess, it's lying low, along with its host."

"How can Leona have survived?" I asked. "I mean, wouldn't the demon be unable to resist killing her?"

"If she made the demon an offer, it's possible the demon decided to spare her life," she said. "Remember that as powerful as demons are, they have certain vulnerabilities. They're dependent on humans to stay within this realm, and as a result, they sometimes have to make compromises."

"What on earth did my grandmother do to anger them, then?" I shook my head. "Aside from banishing them into the deeper afterworld. I mean, she must have done something to attract their attention in the first place."

"My mentor didn't give me all the details," she said. "I'll be sure to ask when he gets back, but for now, you should take this."

She held up a simple grey stone inset with a hole where a sturdy-looking piece of string had been attached. I squinted at the pendant. "What's that?"

"It's a way to call upon me at any time." She pressed the stone into my hand; it was cool to the touch. "Just squeeze the stone if you need me, and I'll be drawn to your side. We're not officially meant to hand these things out to humans, but your case is a special one."

"Okay." I assumed this was a substitute for using the phone, which the Reapers did not seem adept at. "Otherwise, is there anything I can do to prepare myself?"

"Carry sage everywhere you go," she said. "Ask those close to you to do the same."

"And… don't summon ghosts?"

She gave a faint smile. "That too. It's not safe for you to go into the afterworld."

I'd figured, but I'd kind of hoped she'd deal with the problem in a more permanent way, if just to make my grandmother easier to face.

"Thank you for your help," Mum said as the Reaper rose

to her feet. "Do ask your mentor to get in touch when he's back."

"I will." Linnea turned on the spot and—vanished. She melted away into the shadows as if she'd never been here at all.

"Erm… I guess Reapers don't need to use doors." I swivelled to my mother. "That's how she got into the house?"

"Yes."

"Hmm." I gestured to the spot where she'd vanished. "She wasn't what I was expecting."

"No, but neither was your friend Maura."

True, and I wouldn't deny that holding the amulet gave a sense of security I hadn't felt for a while. Knowing a demon might attack at any moment wasn't quite as daunting now I knew I could summon up a Reaper, Pokémon-style, to fight it off. In theory.

I looped the string around my neck. "Why didn't you want her to find Araminta's ghost and banish her? Do you think she *is* still around?"

"She might be," Mum said, "but she won't help us undo the curse, and my mother's ghost is far too volatile to risk letting a Reaper into the building."

"Even if there's a demon around."

"There isn't." Mum's tone warned me to drop the subject. "I did get in touch with a curse-breaker, who told me he can remove the curse from whatever object it was cast upon… *if* the curse was indeed put on an object. If not, and the person responsible is still alive, only they can remove it."

"Nasturtium." It had to be her, but the curse was way down on my priority list if the demon came back.

"We'll see." Her gaze went to the amulet around my neck, and I fingered the cold stone self-consciously.

At least I had one means of defending myself now, but would it be enough?

———

I expected to fight a battle with my mother over whether I should go to the office the following morning. I did not expect to wake up past noon. With a yelp, I bolted out of bed and hurried to get dressed before sprinting downstairs into the living room.

"Why didn't anyone wake me up?" I asked of the world in general. Nobody answered, probably because the only person present was Horace, Mum's cat familiar, who lay napping on the sofa.

"What the hell?" I walked through into the kitchen and found that Kimberly had left me a cooked breakfast in the oven with a note that she'd gone home early. Piper wasn't in the garden, either, though Tansy came running inside when she saw me.

"You're awake." She hopped onto the table. "You were dead to the world when I last saw you."

"No thanks to whoever turned off my alarm." I retrieved my breakfast from the oven. "Did Mum go to the office without me?"

"I think she went to see the curse-breaker," Tansy replied. "She told me to let you rest."

I blew out an irritated breath. "So much for her treating me like someone who can make my own choices."

"The Reaper probably creeped her out." Tansy stole a crumb from the table. "She creeped *me* out, come to that."

Thinking about it, I'd forgotten to pick up the amulet Linnea had given me from my bedside table, but the odds were decently low that I'd need it at the breakfast table. "She's the best chance we've got of stopping the demons. Until her mentor comes back, anyway."

"Since when did Reapers take holidays, anyway?" Tansy asked.

"She mentioned he was meeting the Reaper Council. Not on holiday." The mental image of a shadowy figure wielding a scythe sitting on a surfboard was amusing enough to cheer me up, if nothing else. "Ramsey's at work?"

"Is the sky blue?" Tansy scampered around the table, stealing the crusts from my toast, and generally made a nuisance of herself. "I've been looking for that other squirrel. I think he's left town."

"Nice of him to stay loyal to his witch." I took a bite of slightly overcooked bacon. "I don't buy it. There's something fishy about that whole situation."

"What do you expect? He's a red squirrel." Tansy resumed bouncing up and down on the table, watching the window, while I heard the front door open in the hallway.

I climbed to my feet when Mum entered the kitchen. "Seriously? Don't you think I'm already far enough behind on everything?"

"You needed the rest." She held up a piece of paper—the list of Araminta's enemies—and dropped it onto the kitchen table. "This isn't cursed. The curse-breaker told me to come back when I have something that is."

"Wow." Who spoke to the leader of the Wildwood Coven like that? "I'm guessing curse-breakers aren't known for their people skills."

Mum narrowed her eyes in answer. "I am going to pay a visit to Araminta's daughter."

"Are you?" I asked. "I'd have thought she'd have left Wildwood Heath after Ramsey let her go."

"She still wants her inheritance, I bet," Tansy put in. "She won't leave town without it."

"Right. I forgot." Being arrested was bound to have delayed the process, but she must know she was at risk of being accused of her mother's murder again if nobody else was willing to confess. "She wasn't very cooperative with

Ramsey. Not sure either of us would have much more luck than he did."

"We'll see," she said. "I know which hostel she's staying at, and I think if we talk to her there, she'll have a lot more trouble lying to our faces."

*We.* "You want me to come? Should I bring the sceptre?"

"If you're up for it—yes," she said. "I hope you won't have to use it."

*Me too.* The idea that she'd invited me along without prompting somewhat soothed my annoyance at her for letting me sleep in, though I couldn't say I was particularly keen on another chat with Nasturtium. Or her familiar if he showed his furry face.

"I'll frighten him out of hiding," Tansy announced when I put my plate aside and joined Mum at the door. "Watch and see."

"Don't do anything foolish," Mum told her. "Either of you. Tansy, you should stay behind."

"No, she can come." I beckoned Tansy to follow me out of the house. "If Nasturtium comes out of her room without her familiar, Tansy can go upstairs and see if he's hiding under the bed."

Mum's lips compressed, but she didn't argue any further. We walked the short distance to the Owl's Nest Inn, where I gave Tansy instructions to scale the drainpipe and peer into the windows but not to start any fights unless I gave her the go-ahead.

Inside the inn, Mum confronted the bemused recep- tionist and ordered her to call Nasturtium's room. Within a minute, the woman herself came downstairs, wearing a pink layered dress that made her resemble a wedding cake.

"Head Witch." Nasturtium wore an expression of faint surprise. "I thought you met with an accident."

"You thought wrong." Did she think I was *dead*? If she'd

interacted with my brother in the past week… possibly. *Dammit, Ramsey.* "No thanks to your mother's ghost."

I'd been hoping to startle her into a confession, but she simply laughed. "Came back from the dead, did she? I bet she's angry."

"Not at me." I eyed her suspiciously. "That list you gave us was a fake, wasn't it?"

Her smile faded. "Fake? No…"

"The curse wasn't cast by your mother at all," Mum added. "Was it? It was you."

"I didn't curse anyone," she protested. "How could I? I wasn't even here."

"Your familiar was in town before you showed up," I said. "He was at the Sky Hopper game."

"The what?"

"Oh, come on." I lifted the sceptre, letting its glow wash over the room, and the colour drained from her face. "If we go upstairs, we won't find a red squirrel hiding in your room? He *told* me you sent him to spy on us."

"I…" She trailed off. "He's not mine."

"Really?" Mum asked. "I think we should call the police."

"No!" She shrank back. "I didn't break any laws. I… The squirrel told me he needed me to pretend to be his witch. He said he'd help me convince you to give me my inheritance, but he didn't know your familiar would be so hostile to him."

"You hired a random squirrel to act as your familiar?" I raised a brow at Mum, who glared stonily at Araminta's daughter. "Why would he… Wait, you *spoke* to him?"

"He said someone used a spell to make him able to talk," she mumbled.

"Uh-huh." I glanced at the door, wondering how Tansy was getting along up on the drainpipe. "Yeah, you should come and talk to the police. See if you can get a better story together by then."

"I… Fine." Nasturtium eyed my sceptre, her shoulders slumping. What had changed in the past few days? She hadn't seemed to be afraid of my sceptre during our first meeting, but that had been before Ramsey had arrested her and shut her in the holding cells for three days. That was bound to shake someone up.

"Come on." Mum ordered Nasturtium to walk in front, where she could keep an eye on her, while I lingered behind to fetch my familiar.

"He's not upstairs," Tansy said, jumping off the drainpipe. "I checked every room. Unless you want me to go inside?"

"Not yet," I replied. "Did you hear? Radcliffe isn't Nasturtium's familiar at all. He's a spy."

"I knew it!" she said. "I bet it *was* him who cursed everyone."

"Squirrels can't use magic, though."

"Then maybe he's a squirrel *shifter*." She ran up and down at my side as I followed my mother's lead. "Like that rat."

"Nasturtium claimed someone put a spell on him to make him able to talk." I quickened my pace to catch up with Mum, who was in the process of steering Nasturtium into the police station. "Should we search her hotel room?"

"Yes—do that," she said distractedly. "I'll handle this."

I was curious to know if Nasturtium changed her story, but I was not in the mood to have a bucket of sage dumped on my head, and Tansy was already running back towards the inn. Following, I watched her scurry up the drainpipe again.

She emerged a minute later, declaring Nasturtium's room a squirrel-free zone. "He's not in there. Should I check the other rooms?"

"No… I don't think he's at the inn." Maybe he really had left town, but why go to the trouble of pretending to be Nasturtium's familiar? What did he get out of their supposed deal? "If he didn't come to Nasturtium's rescue while she was in prison, he's not going to show up now."

As for the curse? Yes, one of the other flower club members might have been responsible instead, but my brother would be busy questioning Nasturtium for a while.

"What about Araminta's ghost?" Tansy asked. "If she's hiding in the office, I can scare her out."

"She's a ghost, not a squirrel." Not that the latter was any easier to find. Without any better ideas, I made my way back towards the coven's headquarters, figuring that I might as well check that Aunt Shannon hadn't unleashed any more slug-related disasters while Mum and I had been absent.

Hearing the murmur of voices from behind my office door brought me to a halt, and Tansy sprang onto the crown of my head while I opened the door. To my bemusement, I found Chloe and Grandma engaged in a conversation that petered out when I entered the office.

"Shouldn't you be at home?" Grandma said to me. "Or running errands with your mother?"

"My mother's a bit preoccupied escorting Araminta's daughter to jail," I replied. "Have either of you seen any squirrels?"

"There's one on your head."

"Not Tansy." I ducked my head as she scampered down onto my shoulder. "Turns out the other squirrel was pretending to be Nasturtium's familiar, and he supposedly promised to help her get her inheritance if she went along with the act."

Chloe blinked at me. "Are you sure you're feeling all right?"

"Yes. I'm not delusional. It's just everyone around me who's losing their wits." Since my arms were beginning to ache, I planted the sceptre next to my chair. "What were you two talking about?"

"Ah—Araminta's ghost." Chloe gave an apologetic look to my grandmother. "She hasn't shown up again, but we thought she might be hiding somewhere in here."

"I thought the same, but we can't summon her again." Not without risking another incident. "Unless we loaded the room with sage, but that didn't help us the last time."

"There's too much of that foul stuff already in here," Grandma objected. "I won't have it."

"Or asked a Reaper." Uneasily, I thought of the amulet, which I'd forgotten to pick up on my way out of the house. I didn't *think* I'd need it today, but it'd be embarrassing if I got killed by the demons because of my complete inability to remember where I put anything.

Grandma vanished with an indignant shriek, which I should have seen coming.

Chloe winced. "It's still a touchy subject. I've been trying to keep her calm…"

"She's going to have to deal with it," I said. "Granted, I'm not sure Linnea would appreciate me asking her to find Araminta. Not sure she does house calls."

Maura might offer as a favour, though. After a moment's hesitation, I pulled out my phone and found her number in my contacts.

"What are you doing?" Chloe asked. "Your mother wouldn't want you to do anything risky."

"Calling a Reaper is the opposite of risky. Besides, Maura will be happy to help. I think."

I already owed her several favours for saving my life from the demons, but Mum had already turned down Linnea's offer of help, and Maura was less likely to tell tales on me to the other Reapers. Yes, Linnea had gone against the book when she'd given me the amulet, but when her boss came back, she'd have to go back to doing everything the official way.

Chloe watched with concern as I called Maura's number. The phone rang several times before she picked up.

"Robin." Maura's voice was somewhat crackly, as though she was in a place with a bad signal. "It's not urgent, is it?"

"Kind of?" I hedged. "Well… no. Are you busy?"

"Yes, unfortunately." The crackling intensified. "Haunted houses aren't known for having good reception. Did you speak to the local Reaper since we last ran into one another?"

"No, but I met his apprentice, Linnea," I said. "I was going to ask for your help finding a ghost, but it's okay if you're busy. I'd summon her myself, but the last time I tried, I nearly got dragged out of my body into the afterworld because those demons set a trap for me."

"They did *what?*" Her voice faded and came back. "Sorry —you already have help, right? I can't stay on the line."

"It's all right. I'll ask Linnea." The call cut out before I finished speaking, leaving a fuzzy silence behind. "Or not. It's not her job to find wayward ghosts of ex-flower club leaders."

Nevertheless, I suspected that I'd need a Reaper's help to survive whatever came next.

12

Araminta's ghost was nowhere to be found, though Chloe and I searched all the spare rooms in the coven headquarters. Chloe even talked her way into some of the other witches' offices as well, though I drew the line at disturbing Aunt Shannon. Her office was probably drenched in sage, and besides, I didn't trust her not to get back at me by doing something heinous.

Within an hour of being back at the office, though, part of me hoped she'd set the slugs loose again for a little excitement. I wished I'd stayed with Ramsey to question Nasturtium instead, but when Mum returned to the coven headquarters later that afternoon, she came into my office to inform me that Nasturtium was still stubbornly denying all allegations.

"Araminta's ghost hasn't shown up, either," I told her. "We've checked pretty much everywhere… except for Aunt Shannon's office, that is."

"Oh, *she* doesn't have any ghosts in her office," Mum said. "She's layered the place with sage since the demon incident. Despite all her talk, she won't take any personal risks."

"Figures." That didn't leave many hiding places in the coven headquarters, and it was unlikely that Araminta's ghost had been strong enough to travel further afield. "What's Ramsey's plan, then? If Nasturtium won't confess, I guess he'll have to talk to the other flower club members again."

"Yes, he was saying that when I left," Mum said. "As for that squirrel…"

"Tansy's combing the forest for him." Not that he'd shown his furry little face, either. "Is Nasturtium still claiming he recruited her? Or whatever her story was?"

"Yes, her story is full of holes," Mum said. "She keeps changing her mind. I think it's safe to say he *isn't* her familiar, or else he'd have shown up to help her out."

"She recruited a random squirrel… Why?" We were still missing several pieces of this puzzle, and with Araminta's ghost *and* the squirrel absent, we were sorely short of witnesses who might be able to bring an end to the madness. "Also, have there been any new slug incidents?"

"Three," she replied tersely. "All targeting flower club members."

"Great." The curse was hardly a priority, but leaving it to wreak havoc on the coven members' gardens for the duration was bound to come back to bite us. At least Mum had stopped volunteering me to clean up, not that I'd been capable of doing so while I'd been in a coma. No, the other witches would have to deal with any future slug-related drama on their own.

Grandma remained absent, which meant another day without any magic lessons. I probably needed the recovery time, but when Chloe told me that Mum had postponed the next council meeting until I'd fully recovered, it was hard to quell my feelings of inadequacy.

*Am I up to the job?* The question remained in the back of

my mind throughout the afternoon, though a message from Harvey at the end of the day asking to meet at the Fox's Den lifted my spirits somewhat.

To my great relief, Mum didn't raise too much of a fuss about me going out with Harvey, as long as I agreed to take both the sceptre and the amulet the Reaper had given me.

After the chaos of the past week, there was nothing I wanted more than to spend the evening with him. And Tansy, who was in peak attention-seeking mode and kept stealing bits of food and generally making a nuisance of herself. I finally shooed her off the table when she tried to jump on my cocktail umbrella and nearly upended the whole drink on both of us.

"Tansy!" I swatted at her. "What's wrong with you?"

"I thought it was a squirrel," Tansy piped up from the floor. "It's bright red. That's a danger sign."

"Sorry," I said to Harvey, who'd also got splashed in the process. "That other squirrel has her on edge."

He passed me a napkin. "No worries. What *did* happen to that squirrel, anyway?"

"He vanished." I shrugged. "I don't get whether he was Nasturtium's familiar or otherwise, but I guess her getting arrested freaked him out."

"Or *I* scared him off," Tansy added, having gone back to scrounging crumbs off the floor.

"Weird," he commented. "Sounds like he's a spy for *someone*, if not Nasturtium."

"She can't get a grip on her own story." I returned to my drink. "Tansy suggested he might be a squirrel shifter, but if he was, I wouldn't be able to understand him talking. Besides, that still doesn't explain *why* he attached himself to a witch to help her claim her inheritance if there's nothing obviously in it for him."

"Yeah," he said. "Unless he was working with someone who knew Araminta when she was alive."

"And knew she'd be murdered?" *Or helped them do it?* We were aiming into the dark at this point, but if our little furry friend had been involved in her death, how on earth did you find a squirrel who didn't want to be found? It wasn't like there was a summoning spell for squirrels like there was for ghosts.

"Might be," he said. "Who cursed the coven, though? A squirrel can't use a wand."

"Exactly." I stirred my cocktail absently. "Maybe we need to go back to the flower club for answers."

"We?" he echoed. "Robin, I know your family members like to make everything your problem, but you don't need to get yourself tangled up with Araminta's mad family."

"I tried telling my mother that from the start, but she wouldn't listen." I grimaced. "Besides, Araminta has made her grievances the entire coven's problem. Or someone has."

"Pity the Reaper couldn't help with that." His gaze dropped to the amulet around my neck; I'd told him about Linnea's unexpected visit at the beginning of our date. "I'm glad you have a way to protect yourself now."

"Or have someone else protect me." That was the crux of the problem. My one line of defence involved summoning the Reaper, and if that failed, I was pretty much screwed. "My mother... she doesn't think I'm ready. She thinks I'm too weak."

"I don't think you are." He leaned over the table. "Actually, I think you're one of the strongest people I know."

"Oh, please."

"It's true." He reached for my hand, somewhat hampered by Tansy crawling back up onto my lap. "Seriously, you've had your whole life turned on its head in the space of a few months. It's unreasonable for most people to take that in stride, but you did."

"Not sure I took it in stride." He had a point, though. Most people did not have to adjust to becoming the enemy of a bunch of immortal monsters, and any other ordinary human would have been as inadequately prepared as I'd been. "If you ask me, it's my family who are being unreasonable, but that's no excuse for what I... what I said during our last date." Shame flushed my cheeks at the memory.

"That you didn't intend to stay in Wildwood Heath?" he asked. "I know why you don't want to. It was selfish of me to expect otherwise."

"It's not... It's not that I don't want to." I'd hardly had a moment to think on the subject after my brush with death, but if anything, that experience had strengthened my resolve to iron out any misunderstandings we'd had. "Actually, the time I've spent with you since I came back has been some of the best days of my life."

*He* flushed, which I hadn't expected. "Really?"

"Of course." I frowned at him. "Did you not realise you were the reason I haven't lost my mind yet?"

"Not just me," he protested. "Your dad's been great. Rowan too."

"Obviously, but that doesn't make you any less important to me." I leaned over to him, looked into his eyes. "That's what my family fundamentally doesn't get. Not everything is a competition, and I'm going to do my best to try to make this work out no matter how the Head Witch situation resolves."

*Assuming I survive,* whispered a voice in the back of my head, which I ignored. If the worst happened, I refused to go to my grave with regrets. I'd spent enough of my life pursued by *what-ifs,* shadowed by past failures. No longer.

"*We're* going to make this work out," Harvey corrected.

"I'm not going to put the entire burden on you. That's not my style."

"I know." I managed a smile. "That's what I like about you."

"I'm glad you like me." He tilted his head. "You know… I was wondering if you wanted to come back to mine. After. If your family wouldn't mind."

My mouth parted. "They probably will."

"Of course." His face fell. "I figured, but—"

"But I don't care what they think." I leaned over and kissed him, seized by a fierce determination. I wouldn't allow their fear to dictate my choices, no more than I would my own.

However many times I had to stare death in the face, nothing was worth putting the rest of my life on hold until the Head Witch burden was on someone else's shoulders instead. Tonight, I wouldn't be Head Witch at all.

Tonight, there was only us.

———

Waking up in Harvey's arms was pleasant enough that I could almost ignore my screaming phone alarm on the bedside table in his one-bedroom apartment.

I could sort of understand why he hadn't invited me over before—he'd remarked with a touch of embarrassment that being a Sky Hopper team captain wasn't a high-paying profession unless you were in the big leagues—but I'd reminded him that I was currently staying in my childhood bedroom in the same house as two neurotic family members and their familiars. I was hardly one to judge.

I snuggled into Harvey's arms as my alarm gave another wail, and he groaned. "What *is* that?"

"Tansy must have changed my alarm settings again." I

grabbed the phone and turned it off. "I know, I have to get back home before work, or my mother will send out a search party."

It'd been all well and good to shelve the Head Witch title overnight, but the stream of sunlight through the window reflecting on the sceptre balanced on top of a stack of sports magazines was a reminder that I couldn't evade my responsibilities forever. Or even for one morning. No fewer than three messages from my mother buzzed into my phone while I was getting ready, using my wand to conjure up fresh clothes from home so I didn't have to wear the previous day's outfit like a teenager sneaking back from the house of a guy who her parents didn't approve of.

While Harvey insisted on walking me home, I was less than certain he'd be welcomed with open arms.

"Might be easier if you drop me off at the end of the road," I told him.

"If I walk you home, your mother won't be able to claim I put you in danger," he pointed out. "If we're lucky, we won't run into anyone at all."

"Mum's last message said, 'come outside NOW,'" I replied. "She'll be waiting on the doorstep, I guarantee."

I thought wrong. When I turned into the street, nobody waited in front of Mum's house, but the ominous silence that greeted us at the door was broken by a loud snarling noise.

"Whoa." I came to a halt. "What was that?"

"No idea," Harvey said. "A bear?"

The growl repeated, and my heart sank. "Tansy."

I unlocked the front door with my wand, sprinted through the hallway into the kitchen, and emerged through the doors into the garden.

Two things hit my eyes first. One, the entire garden was covered in slugs, from Mum's prize roses to the towering sunflowers. Two, Tansy had pinned down the other squirrel with both paws, her tail twitching.

"Whoa." I sprinted over to her and stopped short of treading on a slug. "Is that—?"

"I caught him in the woods," Tansy squeaked. "When I chased him here, I found the garden like this."

The squirrel yelped. "No! It wasn't me!"

"Really now." I peered down at him. "How'd you get through the spells I cast around the property?"

"What spells?" His beady eyes bulged when Tansy's tail wagged threateningly. "I didn't see any spells!"

*Where in the world is Mum?* "The whole property was warded." With my sceptre, no less. A squirrel couldn't have possibly undone the defences when he couldn't even use a wand.

"I didn't..." Radcliffe flinched away from Tansy's claws. "I'm not lying!"

"Then you'll tell me why you're here?"

"I'm here to spy on you. Let me go."

"Spy on us for whom?" Nasturtium's face came to mind. "Your so-called witch told me you offered to pretend to be her familiar in exchange for a bribe."

"She said what?" Radcliffe feebly twitched his tail. "She's lying. Let me go."

"I know she's lying, but so are you." I narrowed my eyes. "Unless she was trying to deflect from how she had you murder Araminta. Are you the killer?"

"No!" He wriggled in agitation, but Tansy held him down with both paws again. "No, I'm not a murderer."

"A likely story." I waved my wand, shifting a wave of slugs out of the way so I could step onto the grass to reach him without getting covered in slime. "You're coming with me."

"Don't touch him," Mum said from behind me. "He's cursed."

"What?" Slowly, I swivelled to face my mother.

Mum stood on the patio with her face schooled into deceptive indifference, but I could see the intense anger pulsing behind her eyes and hear the sharp edge to her voice. "The curse wasn't placed on an object at all. It's on him."

"He's… cursed?" Had she lost her wits entirely? Yes, he and the slugs had shown up in the garden at the same time, but putting a curse on a *squirrel* seemed dubious to say the least.

"It's true, isn't it?" Tansy growled at him. "You're cursed. That's why you're spying for her."

"Nasturtium… put a curse on you?" Was that why he was running around on her behalf? It made more sense than him helping her retrieve her inheritance, admittedly, but the woman herself was notably absent. *And who took down the wards?*

Mum lifted her wand, conjuring up a birdcage from somewhere. "Put him in there. We can't have him touching anyone else."

"He won't curse *me*," Tansy said without relinquishing her grip on the squirrel. The fight had gone out of him, though, and he didn't make any effort to resist when Mum levitated him out from underneath Tansy and into the cage.

It was then that I spotted Harvey awkwardly hovering on the patio. He must have followed me—understandably worried—and now I was faced with the awkwardness of him and my mother occupying the same space. Given the state of the garden, the sooner I got him out of here, the better.

"Do you want to hand the squirrel over to Ramsey?" I asked Mum, mostly to keep her attention off Harvey. "Or keep him here?"

"Leave him to me." Mum levitated the cage towards the house, earning a shriek from the occupant, while Tansy came scampering up to my side.

As Mum vanished into the house, I moved closer to Harvey. "Better leave before she finds a way to blame one or both of us for the state of the place."

"Didn't you spend hours putting protective spells around the garden the other day?" he asked.

"I did," I said, "but I guess someone undid them."

"That squirrel," Tansy interjected. "He must have undone the spells during the night."

"He can't have. No curse can get past those boundaries." If it could, the garden would have been hit sooner. We were still missing a few clues, but if Mum was right and the squirrel was the source of the curse, the plague of slugs would soon be over.

As for Araminta's murder? Could Radcliffe and Nasturtium have been responsible for that too? At this point, it was anyone's guess. I couldn't believe I'd missed the possibility of the curse being cast on an animal instead of an object or place, enabling it to easily infiltrate people's gardens without anyone being any the wiser. Nobody was going to blame a squirrel. Except Tansy, of course.

I turned to my familiar. "You were right."

"Obviously." She twitched her tail. "Other red squirrels are *never* trustworthy."

A door slammed inside the house, and I grimaced. "Harvey, you'd better go before Mum comes back from handing our fluffy intruder to Ramsey."

"Good call." He gave me a hug. "See you later?"

"I'll message you." I led him to the back of the garden, figuring he'd be safer escaping the house through the forest while Mum was still storming around.

When I got back to the house, I found that Mum had planted the squirrel's cage on the coffee table in the living room. Horace the cat hissed at its occupant from the sofa, and Radcliffe cowered in the cage's corner away from Mum's familiar.

"When did you notice the wards were down?" I asked Mum, deciding to face the inevitable. "I mean—he must have had help. A squirrel can't have removed them alone."

"I'm aware," she said through gritted teeth. "Nobody else was caught on the property, but if your familiar hadn't been here, we'd never have caught the culprit."

I heard the implication loud and clear, but she was wrong. "If you didn't hear the intruder, I certainly wouldn't have. Even if I'd been here."

My body tensed in anticipation of her reply, but she simply picked up the birdcage in one hand. "I am going to take the intruder to the police."

"Do you want me to use the sceptre to redo the wards?" I gestured in the direction of the back garden. "Or should I… erm, go to work?"

I didn't have to be at the office for another hour or more, but I figured that redoing the wards around the property ought to take precedence. And getting rid of the slugs, though I wasn't sure she wanted me touching her garden. I could hardly ruin flowers that had already been chewed to ribbons, but leaving the slugs to eat their way through the garden didn't appeal, either, especially if Aunt Shannon or her familiar had been watching from the other side of the fence.

When Mum didn't answer, I said, "I'll call Piper. She'll fix the garden."

At least she got paid for it, though I didn't envy her the task of getting rid of hundreds of magically created slugs.

"No," Mum said in firm tones. "Nobody outside of our family is to come into the house until the security spells have been redone."

"Oh, come on, Piper's proven herself trustworthy over

and over again." Given Mum's expression, she wasn't going to budge on that one. "Fine. I'll do it all myself."

While Mum left the room with the squirrel's cage in hand, Tansy gave a last growl at the other squirrel and then followed me back to the garden.

"You don't want to go with them?" I asked her.

"No," she said. "Your mother won't let him escape, and I don't trust him not to have brought friends."

"Whoever undid the wards." A chill raced down my spine, though I'd put on the amulet Linnea had given me as soon as I'd woken up. Between that and the sceptre, I was reasonably sure I could handle *most* threats… if they were human.

I surveyed the garden, not quite sure where to start. The slugs would impede my ability to reach the boundaries of the fence, but moving them would require finding another pile of buckets, at least until Mum managed to get Nasturtium to undo the curse and make them disappear entirely.

Tansy scampered onto the fence. "I'm going to watch out for more intruders."

"All right." I was already regretting not going with Mum instead, but I picked a starting point and raised the sceptre to begin casting the boundary spell.

That was when I saw the brightly dressed figure approaching the garden from the forested path behind.

Nasturtium.

13

"You." I lowered the sceptre and walked to face her at the back fence. "Come to collect your squirrel? He's already gone."

Wasn't she supposed to be locked in the holding cells? How had she escaped? Questions swarmed my mind, but they fled when I saw the familiar flat blackness in her eyes.

"Robin." Tansy hissed. "She's…"

"I know."

She was possessed by a demon. *Oh no.*

"Robin." The demon smiled using Nasturtium's mouth. "We meet again."

"If you say so." I couldn't even tell which demon it was, as there'd been two—one possessing Leona and one that Maura had sent packing—but only now did it sink in how quiet the garden was. While normally, I'd expect the local wildlife to respond to my rising emotions, nothing stirred; every animal except Tansy had fled in the demon's wake. And the slugs, of course, but they weren't real.

"Really, Robin, my feelings are hurt," said the demon. "You don't remember me?"

"I'm face blind. And you don't even *have* a face." Though if Leona was still alive somewhere, this demon was more likely to be the second, the one we'd banished. "You're the demon that Maura sent to the afterworld?"

"That wasn't very nice of her," said the demon, "but your Reaper friend isn't here now, is she?"

"That doesn't matter." Around my neck was the amulet Linnea had given me. One touch, and I'd be able to summon her to my side.

The demon laughed. "You think she's going to come to help you?"

*She?* He couldn't possibly know about Linnea, so he must mean Maura. "How long have you been possessing Nasturtium, out of curiosity?"

"Not long," the demon said. "Her thoughts are dull enough that I can only stand being in her head long enough to pass on this message to you."

"What message?" My body tensed. "You... you killed Araminta, didn't you?"

The demon simply laughed, a chilling sound, and adrenaline flooded my body. *Whether he killed her or not, he's certainly killed people before, and he'd be more than happy to let me be one of them.*

I wasn't entirely sure why I was calling the demon a "he" —perhaps because his voice struck me as starkly masculine and his mannerisms contrasted with Nasturtium's bright clothes. Her dress was somewhat grubbier after a night in jail, but she couldn't have been possessed then. The police station was surrounded by sage, which suggested she'd escaped of her own accord somehow, but when? Had she run into Mum and Ramsey on the way out? Surely not—the demon would never have let them pass without possessing one of them—but worry for them added to the cocktail of emotions churning inside me.

The demon's eyes were locked on me, taunting. Yet he hadn't moved. The security spells might be down, but sage encircled the property, and I carried enough in my pockets that possessing *me* was out of the question. All he had left to do was fling insults at me and try to goad me into leaving the security of my mother's house... or else wait for Mum and Ramsey to come back.

"Go on," I pressed. "What's this message?"

The demon gave another laugh. "You should be careful who you place your trust in."

"I don't have time for this." I lifted the sceptre and cast a freezing charm. The demon made no attempt to resist, but it was Nasturtium whose body went rigid, turning into a human statue.

"Nice try." The demon's voice spoke through her mouth, but her lips didn't move. Man, that was creepy. The demon would be able to move, of course, but only if it let go of its host. "If you're going to be like *that*, Robin, I'll have to pick another host instead. Which friend of yours will you offer as a sacrifice, I wonder?"

Darkness coalesced behind Nasturtium as the demon released her, and panic surged in my chest. *My friends. No.*

I would not allow the demon to touch any of them.

I reached for the pendant with my free hand and closed my fingers around the cool stone, squeezing tight. One touch should do it, Linnea had said—but the demon was already moving away from Nasturtium. Darkness surged across the forest path.

"Hey!" I waved the sceptre wildly, not thinking, and a wave of slugs rose into the air. They had no effect on the demon, of course, but Nasturtium gave a startled cry when they landed on top of her. Oops. I'd undone the freezing spell as well, but the noise momentarily distracted the demon.

The Reaper appeared, a shadowy figure outlined in darkness, and the demon vanished in the same instant.

Linnea surveyed the garden, her gaze lingering on the terrified Nasturtium. "Looks like I got here just in time."

"The demon's gone." I pointed at the spot where it'd vanished. "Where—?"

"It's in the afterworld. I'll find it." The Reaper disappeared, sucked into the darkness she'd walked out of, and Nasturtium staggered back, her face paling. She didn't seem to have noticed half the slugs had landed in her hair—which served her right if you asked me.

"Hey." I took a step closer to her. "Snap out of it."

Tansy, who'd hidden behind a flowerpot when the demon had appeared, came running into view. "Want me to bite her?"

Nasturtium lifted her head, eyes brimming with fear. "Where am I?"

"Don't pull that one on me," I snapped. "Did you know that demon possessed you? Or was that part of the plan?"

"I was possessed?" She swayed on her feet, looking as though she was about to pass out. "That's not possible."

"It is, and you're lucky to be alive," I told her. "You're also supposed to be in the holding cells. Did the demon help you escape?"

"I…" She flinched. "Radcliffe helped, but you caught him, didn't you?"

"Your squirrel set you free?" After she'd put a curse on him? "I guess the demon saw you were heading towards my house and couldn't resist."

"Your squirrel's off to jail," Tansy told her. "And you're going to join him."

"I should point out that the jail is one of the few places in town surrounded by sage," I added to her. "No demons can get in there."

The same applied to my dad's cottage, but the demon might have gone after any other target. Harvey. Rowan. Piper. I had too many people I couldn't afford to lose, and while I knew Linnea would do her best to find the demon, I wouldn't rest until he was banished once again.

"That's right." Tansy beckoned with her tail. "Come with us."

Nasturtium followed meekly enough, slugs falling out of her hair with every step. Tansy helped me herd her towards the back gate to the forest path, but I'd forgotten the noise would have attracted attention.

Aunt Shannon's head popped up over the fence, and she grinned widely. "Curse finally got you, did it?"

"Were *you* the one who removed the protective spells around the house?" My shoulders tensed, and I lifted the sceptre in both hands. "I don't have time for your nonsense. There's a demon on the loose."

"Really." She walked out onto the forest path, eyeing Nasturtium. "Who's this?"

"A criminal." I nudged her in front of me and began to walk. "You can do everyone a favour and stay out of the way."

Aunt Shannon wouldn't give up that easily. She tailed me down the forest path like a particularly annoying shadow. "I know what I saw in your garden. A *Reaper*. Do the rest of the coven know?"

"I don't have time to make a dozen phone calls," I said testily. "You can go ahead and do that yourself if you want to risk being turned into demon bait."

No doubt she'd find a way to twist this situation to her advantage, but at this precise minute, I couldn't bring myself to give a crap. Aunt Shannon finally stopped tailing us when Tansy and I led Nasturtium out of the forest.

We followed the main road to the police station, where Julian goggled at me when I pushed Nasturtium ahead of me into the lobby. "I found your escaped prisoner. Where's Ramsey?"

"Here." Ramsey himself came running out of his office, followed by my mother. "The security questions—"

"I'm not possessed, but *she* was." I gave Nasturtium another push. "Linnea went after the demon. When did you notice your prisoner was missing?"

"Shortly after I arrived." He produced a pair of handcuffs from a pocket. "I had people searching for her. I assumed she'd go back to her mother's house..."

"That's probably where she was when the demon possessed her," I guessed. "Or on her way to my house. He had a built-in excuse."

"The demon." Mum's nostrils flared. "Where is it?"

"I don't know, do I?" I indicated the amulet. "I called for help, and Linnea will handle the rest. Where's that squirrel?"

Neither he nor his fellow conspirator was at the top of our priority list, but someone had summoned the demon in the first place.

"The squirrel is in your brother's office," Mum replied. "I'm intending to take him to a curse-breaker."

"He didn't confess to conspiring with demons?" I queried. "Or murdering Araminta?"

Nasturtium whimpered as Ramsey tugged her through the lobby towards the holding cells, but a nagging voice in my head told me she hadn't been the instigator of this. I needed to find Araminta's ghost to get the rest of the story, but that would have to wait until after the demon was dealt with. Pulling out my phone, I fired off messages to Harvey, Piper, and Rowan, warning them to lie low. *Please be quick, Linnea.*

My phone started buzzing with a call, and I was surprised to see Maura's name pop up. *Is she in the area?* I hoped so, because two Reapers were better than one, especially if Leona showed her face too.

"Hey." I took the call and moved away from the others to properly hear beyond the crackle of static in the background. "Can you talk now? We have a demon-related situation here. The other Reaper's in town, but—"

"The other Reaper," she interrupted. "Did you say her name was Linnea?"

"Yes," I said. "Linnea. She's looking for the—"

"No." She spoke quickly. "I asked my Reaper friend, someone who's involved with the council, and your local Reaper isn't at a meeting. He's disappeared."

"What?" My heart missed a beat. "Reapers can't disappear."

"Apparently, they can," she said. "I don't know the details, but—he mentioned something about a rogue apprentice."

"Linnea?" Impossible. "We spoke in the afterworld. She saved my life. Stopped Araminta's ghost from pulling me out of my body."

"Ghosts can't do that, Robin," Maura said. "Nor can demons. Reapers, though… *they* can."

"No." She couldn't be right. Linnea was chasing the demon for me. She'd given me the protective amulet…

"I know she probably made herself seem trustworthy," Maura said, "but there are rogue Reapers out there. The sort who target people who wouldn't know the difference between them and a real Reaper."

"Why?" My blood ran cold. "She didn't threaten me. She came to help."

"I honestly don't know what her agenda is, but she'll have one." Maura swore. "I'll come and help, but frankly, I don't know what the odds are of me being able to take out a full-blown rogue Reaper."

"You don't have to come." My hand gripped the phone,

slick with sweat. What were the odds of *me* being able to take out a full-blown rogue Reaper? Even one without a… Wait, Linnea didn't have a scythe, at least, but if Maura was right, she'd *pulled me out of my body.*

"I will," she said. "Give me an hour, tops. If you see her again, I wouldn't confront her. Pretend you're still not in the know. There's no telling what she might be planning."

"But what about—?"

Her voice crackled, and then the call cut out.

"Robin." Mum peered at my face. "Who were you speaking to?"

"Maura called me." I lowered the phone. "She told me Linnea isn't a real Reaper. She's a rogue, and her mentor isn't on sabbatical. He's missing."

"Maura said that, did she?"

"I don't know what to believe, either," I admitted, "but I trust Maura, and she told me that a ghost couldn't have pulled me out of my body. A Reaper, though…"

"What is it?" Ramsey came out of the holding cells, smelling strongly of sage. "Where's the demon?"

"Not the demon," I said. "Linnea. Maura told me she's an impostor and a rogue who's out to take advantage of us."

"Someone say my name?" said Linnea.

14

The Reaper stood in the doorway to the police station, a shadowy figure placed between us and the way out. Tansy growled and leapt onto my shoulder, while Linnea took a slow, deliberate step forwards over the line of sage across the doorway as though to emphasise that none of our defences could keep her out. She wasn't a demon. She was something more.

Ramsey strode to my side. "You. What do you want?"

Linnea raised a brow. "What's with the tone?"

"Where's the demon?" I demanded. "Did you let it go?"

My words washed over her, and a ripple of emotion I didn't recognise passed over her face, settling into a mixture of resignation and grim determination. "Who told you? The ghost?"

*What ghost?* "Who, Araminta? Is she with you too?"

"Never mind." She glided forwards, into the lobby, her feet skimming the floor as if she were a ghost herself. "Sorry about this. It's nothing personal."

"Nothing personal?" I lifted the sceptre, but the shadows cloaking her were a world apart from the magic I had at my own fingertips, and she didn't so much as give me a second glance. Her attention was trained on Mum instead.

Mum's wand was already in her hand, but the Reaper vanished into darkness and reappeared in the time it took to blink. Then her hand was on my mother's arm, and the darkness swallowed them both.

"Mum." I took a step forwards, numb with shock, shouts echoing in the background as the other police officers ran into the lobby to see what was going on. "What the hell was that?"

Ramsey recovered first. "It's obvious. That Reaper has an agenda of her own, and she intends to use our mother as a hostage."

"For what reason?" She hadn't said a word. *It's nothing personal?* Was it the Head Witch she had a grudge against, like the demons? Why go after Mum instead?

"Your guess is as good as mine." White-faced with fury, Ramsey moved towards the other officers and began barking commands at them. Some left the station, while others moved into the holding cells, but I hovered on the spot, torn. If Linnea had had no intention of recapturing the demon, it must still be roaming around the town, hunting my friends. She might even have been the person who'd summoned it in the first place, and I had no way to banish the demon on my own.

Unless I called another Reaper.

I fished out my phone and found several missed calls from Harvey. Oh, crap. Heart sinking, I moved towards the door, but Ramsey called after me. "Don't go outside the sage."

"Harvey's—" I choked off, panic writhing in my chest. "The demon told me—he's going after my friends next."

"Our mother needs our help too." Ramsey held his own phone in his hand, clenched in a white-knuckled grip. "I'm sending out a team."

"From where?" Reapers could cross entire countries in a single step, thanks to the afterworld, and none of us had any hope of catching up to Linnea unless we had another Reaper on our side.

My heart gave a jump when I spied Harvey approaching the police station. "Harvey—do you have any sage? Are you okay?"

"Robin." Ramsey spoke quietly. "Look at his eyes."

The doors slid open, revealing the demon's flat-eyed stare from behind Harvey's eyes.

"No!" A scream tore from my throat, and Tansy leapt forwards in a blur of red. I watched, horrified, as she landed on top of Harvey's head and dug her claws in.

"Let go of him!" she squeaked.

"Tansy, stop!" I reached into my pocket for one of the pouches of sage and flung it at Harvey. Tansy leapt clear, landing on all four paws on the desk, and the sage hit Harvey full in the face.

Harvey staggered back as the demon flew out of his body, blurring into a patch of darkness. A bright flash of light ignited, and the sage I'd thrown at the demon rose into the air again, circling it.

Ramsey approached the demon with his wand held aloft, expertly levitating the sage in a perfect circle and leaving the demon no route to escape.

"Whoa." Impressive. He'd been practising some new tricks, evidently, but would even that hold the demon indefinitely?

Harvey fell to his knees and wrenched my attention away from the demon. Alarmed, I crouched beside him. "Harvey. Speak to me."

Harvey lifted his head, horror and confusion warring in his eyes. "Robin... the demon..."

"I got the demon out of you, don't worry." I gestured to

the sage, which had settled into a circle on the floor, keeping the demon caged. "You. Demon. Were you working with that Reaper?"

The demon gave a cold laugh. "Who else would have been able to summon me?"

"What's going on?" Harvey pushed shakily to his feet. "The demon… Isn't the Reaper supposed to be dealing with it herself?"

"We thought wrong." I didn't want to say too much in front of the demon, but Harvey had already been dragged into this mess. "The Reaper's not who she seems. She summoned the demon and took Mum as a hostage."

"She took your mother?" Harvey's gaze fixed on the amulet around my neck. "Doesn't that summon the Reaper?"

"Only if she wants to listen." For all I knew, she'd be able to use the same amulet to drag me out of my body again like she'd done before. With a shudder, I grabbed the string and looped it over my head, tossing the amulet onto the desk. Julian, who I'd quite forgotten was there, leapt out of his seat as though I'd thrown a grenade at him, while Ramsey stepped in and picked up the amulet himself.

"I'll deal with this," he said. "You—Robin—"

"Don't finish that sentence." My body trembled with adrenaline, one hand clutching the sceptre and the other reaching for my phone, while I kept an eye on the demon, knowing it would be assessing our every move for an opportunity to escape.

Unless we banished it.

Scrolling to Maura's name, I hit the call button. The call went straight to voicemail. I swore loudly. "Maura's not available. Anyone else have a Reaper on speed dial?"

I knew how to cast a banishment spell, but banishing a demon was a world apart from banishing a ghost, and even Maura hadn't been able to keep this one away for long.

Within the darkness, the demon shifted. Watching for my next move.

"Well?" I addressed the shadow within the sage. "You aren't going anywhere, so if you wanted to tell us your Reaper friend's plans, it'll save us a lot of bother."

"You're in no position to make threats," said the demon. "You're nothing more than a pretender of a Head Witch."

"I *am* Head Witch." I pointed the sceptre at the swirling darkness. "Out of curiosity, why *did* you murder Araminta?"

"Why do you think?" the demon asked. "More to the point, why do you care? You hated her."

"So did everyone else, which I guess is why Linnea chose her as a target."

The demon didn't contradict my words, which voiced a suspicion that had been brewing in my mind. Together, the Reaper and the demon had instigated Araminta's murder, knowing that it would cause enough of a fuss that the coven would summon back Araminta's ghost and give the Reaper an opportunity to gain my trust. Since the local Reaper had been instrumental in banishing the demons the first time around, it made sense that they'd want him out of the way.

Whether Leona and the other demon had been involved was debatable, but I'd bet my sceptre that they were. Which meant there was a chance we'd have to deal with *two* demons soon enough.

"And her daughter?" I asked. "Were you helping Nasturtium?"

"Enough." Ramsey stepped in, his expression mildly deranged. "If we can't banish the demon, we have one option."

"Which is...?" I asked sceptically.

"We're evacuating the police station." He indicated the door. "Everyone wait outside."

*Not the prisoners too?* I swallowed down my questions

when the demon let out a high, chilling laugh. If Ramsey tried to move its sage prison, the demon might seize the chance to escape, so it was theoretically less of a risk to leave the demon imprisoned inside the station until a genuine Reaper showed up.

That didn't mean I wanted Harvey to stay in the same room. "C'mon." I beckoned him outside. "Let's humour him."

Harvey reluctantly followed me out the door. "Is he going to let the prisoners out?"

"Unlikely," I replied. "The cells are far enough away from the demon, I think, but the other officers will have to hang around outside until the coast is clear."

"Robin…" Harvey peered into my eyes. "Are you okay? Really?"

"Of course I'm not okay," I said shakily. "Mum got captured by a rogue Reaper, and the *other* Reaper isn't answering her phone. If we can't use Maura's help to travel through the afterworld, how are we supposed to find her?"

"A ghost?" Harvey suggested. "Not that I'm an expert, but they're in the afterworld too."

"Right." That was a starting point, a slim one, but there must be a way. I had the sceptre, and it was supposed to be capable of anything.

Nothing would stop me from finding my mother. Not even a false Reaper.

15

Ramsey emerged from the police station, pursued by a group of confused officers asking questions and generally drawing too much attention.

"Stay there," Ramsey told them. "Stop anyone else from getting into the station. Yes, that includes your fellow officers..."

I tuned him out, thinking hard. *The ghosts...* Would they be able to find the Reaper? That would depend on how far she'd gone. Where she'd taken Mum.

*Mum.* Impatience burned within me, tempered by worry for my friends. And Harvey.

"Harvey." I turned to him, my heart contracting. "Please... can you go and find somewhere to lie low? Get some sage, make sure you stay where the demons can't get at you. I don't trust them not to try to use you against me again."

He shook his head. "I can't let you go after that demon without me."

"She won't be alone," said a squeaky voice that I at first thought belonged to Tansy. Then I spied Radcliffe scurrying out of the police station. "I'll help."

"How'd you get out of your cage?" Ramsey demanded.

"I'm a squirrel."

"Get back in there!" Tansy jumped down in front of him, her tail puffed up. "Now."

Radcliffe lifted himself upright. "I want to make it up to you. I want to help."

"How do we know you aren't working with the demon yourself?" I asked. "You can't be possessed."

"I'm also cursed," the other squirrel. "I can use that to help you, can't I?"

"No." Would a Reaper be terrified of magically created slugs? Unlikely. "No, you're staying behind. With Nasturtium."

The police station doors slid open, and Nasturtium herself stepped outside. "I can help too."

"You," said Ramsey, "are supposed to be in the holding cells."

"There's a *demon* in the lobby." She shuddered. "I'm not staying in there and waiting to be possessed. Anyway, I can find my mother's ghost myself."

I raised a brow at her. "You spoke to Araminta?"

"She appeared to me at home," Nasturtium admitted. "Yelled at me for stealing her curse idea."

"When was this?" Araminta was hardly trustworthy, but as long as I couldn't get hold of Maura, ghosts were my only contacts on the other side.

"Erm… last night." She eyed Ramsey beseechingly. "You can lock me up again afterwards. I don't mind."

"A likely story." She wasn't in league with the demons, though, and we couldn't afford to waste any more time by trying to drag her back to the holding cells. "If you insist, you can come with us to find the rogue Reaper. It's your funeral."

Ramsey opened his mouth as though he intended to

disagree, but he must have decided it wasn't worth the effort too. "Come on, then."

He turned his back on his fellow officers' questions and complaints and overtook me, leading the way to the coven headquarters on swift feet. Behind him, Harvey kept pace with me until we reached the doors.

"I'll be okay," I said quietly. "Trust me. It'll be easier on both of us if you lie low where the demon *and* the Reaper can't find you."

His mouth turned down at the corners. "I don't want you to get hurt again."

"I could say the same for you." I lifted the sceptre. "I have this. Remember?"

He leaned over and pulled me against him, kissing me hard. "I trust you. Please... be safe."

"I will." Reluctantly, I pulled away from Harvey. "I'll be back before you know it."

*Or dead.* Best not think about that outcome. Ramsey had already entered the coven headquarters, so I strode in behind him and opened my office door on a startled Chloe.

"Where's Grandma?" I spied her ghostly figure hovering near the back of the room and continued onward breathlessly. "The Reaper is a fake, and she's captured Mum. Grandma, I assume you know why."

My grandmother floated towards me, wearing a peevish expression. "I most certainly do not."

"Linnea summoned the demon," I told her. "Did the coven do anything to anger any Reapers that I should know about?"

"Not that I recall." She pursed her lips. "Captured your mother? You'd better go and rescue her, hadn't you?"

"I would if I knew where to find her." I turned to Ramsey, who stood in the doorway with Nasturtium hovering behind him. "They could have gone literally anywhere. We need a ghost's help. Have you seen Araminta? I know she's still around."

If she'd been paying house calls to Nasturtium, she must have been a stronger ghost than I'd realised, but that was beside the point. When Grandma didn't answer, I spoke, addressing the room at large. "Araminta was murdered by Linnea, the Reaper, who intended to distract the coven."

Araminta's ghost appeared in a flash of light. "You *what?*"

"She killed you," I told her. "Linnea did. The Reaper's apprentice... Well, she's not really an apprentice."

"I *knew* those Reapers were untrustworthy," Grandma said triumphantly. "What did I tell you?"

"Linnea isn't an official one," I reminded her. "And we can't find Mum without the help of a genuine Reaper."

"Did you forget I'm a ghost?" Grandma lifted her chin. "I can go anywhere."

"You can't go further than our house," I pointed out. "Araminta...*you* can, can't you?"

It did seem odd that Araminta had more mobility than my grandmother, a former Head Witch. Had the Reaper unintentionally super-charged her ghost somehow when she'd used her to fake the attempt on my life?

"Obviously," Araminta replied. "Where is my killer? Let me at her."

"I don't know where she is. That's the problem." I took in a breath. "But you can find her. You've seen her before... She appeared in the afterworld when you first showed up here at headquarters."

Araminta paled, or as far as was possible for a ghost. "*That* Reaper?"

"Who'd you think I meant?" A chill rose to my skin at the memory of her cold hands on my skin, pulling me out of my body. "She killed you and tried to blame you for the attempt on my life. Then she took my mother hostage. You can find her in the afterworld, can't you?"

She wrapped her ghostly arms around herself. "I'm not going to put myself at risk."

"What risk?" My heart sank in my chest. She might be a ghost, but there were fates worse than death. The time I'd spent around Reapers had taught me that.

"Don't be such a wet blanket," Grandma snapped at Araminta. "Help them."

I stared at her, surprised. "You *want* to find Linnea?"

"Don't give me that look," she said. "We both know that if you don't find that Reaper, your mother isn't coming back."

My heart contracted. "I know. Araminta, can you try to find her? You don't have to fight. We just need directions."

She pouted. "Fine, but if I end up killed again, it'll be on your conscience."

"You can't be killed twice." Though I wouldn't put anything past a Reaper. "You only have to lead the way to her."

"It's dark and terrifying over there." But Araminta's gaze zoned out, her ghostly body going completely still, her eyes fixed at a point somewhere in the distance. After a short pause, she blinked back to the present. "I can sense the right direction… I think."

"Better than nothing." I gestured to the door. "Lead the way."

I couldn't believe I was relying upon the ghost of the deceased flower club leader to save my mother's life, but it wasn't even the most surprising event of the day. Araminta drifted out of the office, skirting close enough that her cold touch brushed against my arm and made me suppress a shudder. Grandma didn't follow, but I didn't expect her to; she was limited in her ability to travel long distances and terrified of the Reaper besides.

Araminta drifted out of the coven's headquarters, and Ramsey and I hurried behind, with Nasturtium reluctantly bringing up the rear.

"She must be stronger than a regular ghost," I muttered to my brother. "I guess she picked up on some of the Reaper's power."

"I wouldn't count on it lasting." Ramsey marched ahead of me; being taller, he could more easily keep up with the ghost, who'd picked up the pace, her ghostly feet skimming the ground as she glided towards the entrance to the forest.

"She's in the Wildwood?" No way. She couldn't be that close, not unless she *wanted* us to find her.

Araminta moved even faster instead of answering, and I glimpsed two red furry shapes pursuing her. The two squirrels raced alongside one another; strangely, Tansy wasn't fighting off the other squirrel or chasing him. They must have come to a temporary truce to help rescue Mum. *That or Tansy's keeping him under close watch.*

The Wildwood swallowed us up, trees seeming to draw tighter as we followed the ghost's lead. All too soon, the scent of sage warned me that we were going past the protective boundary my brother had put around the woodland encircling my family's home, and once we were outside, we'd be entirely vulnerable to any demon that might be waiting. Yet Mum was out there, too, and though she might surrender her coven leader title rather than admitting it, she needed our help.

Despite it being the middle of the day, the forest darkened the further we walked, and foreboding washed over me as I recalled the vision in the Seeing Stone. Hadn't I seen something similar, a scene of myself walking through the forest into oncoming darkness?

I shook off the thought. In the vision, I'd been alone, not accompanied by my brother, two squirrels, a scheming witch, and her ghostly mother. I could guarantee even the Seeing Stone couldn't conjure up an image *that* bizarre.

Araminta's ghost came to a sudden halt. "No... don't make me go any further!"

Darkness encased us. Pitch-black, impenetrable, and chilling. *The afterworld.*

I squinted into the dark, my gaze picking out something shaped oddly like... a house. It might simply be an illusion, but through a squarish shape that resembled a window, I glimpsed two figures moving around inside the house-like construction.

The Reaper... and Mum.

Ramsey hissed out a warning, but my patience flew out the window at the sight of my mother inside the Reaper's domain.

"Hey!" I shouted, running towards the house. I called on my family's magic, but we were in the afterworld, where nothing was alive, and no animals answered my call.

The Reaper's head turned towards me, but Mum didn't budge. What had the Reaper done to her? From the angle, she appeared to be standing upright, but she gave no reaction to my words. Nor to my sceptre, which I waved, casting a perfect freezing charm.

Linnea moved fluidly to block my path, the spell merely vanishing into the surrounding darkness. *Dammit.* Evidently, my sceptre didn't work in the illusion the Reaper had conjured up.

"I warned you," she told me. "You didn't have to follow us."

"Like hell," I spat. "She's my mother. Why in hell did you kidnap her?"

"She's the coven leader." The Reaper's shadowy form appeared to glow around the edges, though she remained etched in darkness. "The leader of the same coven who murdered *my* mother."

Despite myself, I stared at her. "What?"

"You heard me," she said. "I became a Reaper to get her back, but I never forgot what the Wildwoods did."

There had to be some context I was missing here, but more prevalent was my concern for Mum. Her expression, now I could see her more clearly behind the "window" of the Reaper's house, was as blank as a slate. "My mother isn't to blame for whatever happened to your family, but if you hurt *my* family, I'll call whoever in authority can make you pay for your crimes."

"You're not a part of this, Head Witch," she said. "Your brother holds no authority here, and neither does anyone else save for myself."

Ramsey, who'd lifted his wand, ignored her. His attention was trained on Mum. "You tricked the Reapers into taking you in… for revenge? What did you do to the real Reaper?"

Good question. Could Reapers permanently die? I wasn't clear on that one, but it seemed impossible that they could be fooled into teaching their secrets to someone who intended to use those skills against them.

She gave a tight smile. "What do you think?"

"He's not the only one you killed." I risked a glance behind me to see if Araminta was still around, but she seemed to have dropped her own revenge quest in favour of hiding behind a tree. *Figures.* I knew the Reaper terrified her, and with good reason, but Nasturtium was nowhere to be seen either. That left Ramsey, me, and—

The two squirrels. I lifted my head, seeing a flash of red amid the darkness, a moment before the pair of them leapt at Linnea.

*"Tansy!"*

Part of me expected the squirrels to fly straight through Linnea's shadowy body—but though she didn't look quite solid, she was more alive than anything else in this place.

Linnea staggered back in surprise when the two squirrels landed on top of her, and Ramsey sprinted past the Reaper to our mother's side. When his hands closed around her upper arms, she didn't fight. Didn't react at all, in fact.

Linnea snarled, shadows surging outwards from her body and causing the squirrels to leap away from her with squeaks of alarm. As she ran towards Ramsey, I raised the sceptre and leapt at her.

While its magic had no effect in darkness, being hit on the head with a massive stick had the same effect on a Reaper as it would a regular person. The sceptre collided with her forehead with a loud thud, and as she staggered away, Ramsey seized her arms from behind.

When the clink of metal followed, I stared at him. "Did you just handcuff the Reaper?"

"That won't work," Linnea snarled, fighting against his hold. "I'm not human, you fool."

"These handcuffs aren't designed for humans." He tugged on her hands, and Linnea stumbled, shock flitting across her face. "See?"

*Where'd he get those?* Questions burst to life in my head, only to fizzle when I locked eyes with Mum. She retained her blank expression and didn't move to join us outside the Reaper's house. Heart in my throat, I hurried to her side. When I touched her, her skin was icy cold. "Mum. Speak to me."

Not a word. I caught Ramsey's gaze, which reflected my own alarm, though he swiftly tamped down his emotions. "It's got to be some effect of being in this place. It'll fade when we're back home."

*Will it?* Gingerly, I took Mum by the arm and tugged her forwards, out of the house-like structure. Its shadowy edges seemed even less defined than before, and as Mum and I moved away, it collapsed in on itself, the patch of darkness shrinking. The Wildwood became visible again, trees popping up out of the gloom until nothing remained of the darkness at all. Even the Reaper appeared more humanlike than before, as if the handcuffs my brother had used on her had somehow sapped her powers.

I definitely needed to ask him about that later, but when I coaxed Mum to take another step forwards, she suddenly keeled over. I caught her in my arms before she fell, staggering under her weight. Ramsey moved forwards, but he was hampered by the handcuffed Reaper and couldn't help as I lowered Mum's limp body to the ground.

"No. *No.*" I felt for a pulse. There was one, but faint, and raw fear pulsed through my body. "You. Linnea. What did you do to her?"

"I didn't kill her," she snarled between her teeth. "Humans aren't supposed to stay in the afterworld for long. This wouldn't have happened if she'd cooperated, and I'll do worse to *you* when I next have the chance, mark my words."

"You aren't going to have another chance." Ramsey pushed her in front of him, causing her handcuffs to rattle. "You'll see."

I remained kneeling beside my mother, unsure what else to do. Now that the adrenaline of the fight was starting to drain out of me, my hands trembled so much that I could hardly keep my grip on the sceptre. Forcing myself to my feet, I scanned the trees and spied Nasturtium lurking out of sight, along with her ghostly mother. Next to them, the two squirrels appeared to be arguing with one another, though they stopped when I approached. "Tansy, can you fetch someone to help with Mum?"

"I don't want to let *him* out of my sight." She indicated Radcliffe with her tail.

"Oh, you're back to being enemies again." I glared at him

then at Nasturtium. "As for you, you promised to hand your-self back over to the police."

"I promised no such thing," Araminta announced.

"I wasn't talking to you." I cast a levitation charm on Mum's unconscious body. It wasn't perfect, but it'd help me get her back behind the safety of the town's boundaries. "Tansy?"

"All right." She scampered past my brother, who watched our exchange with a furrowed brow. He had his phone in one hand—calling backup, I guessed—though the other retained a grip on the Reaper's handcuffs.

We walked, me levitating Mum, him leading the Reaper. I didn't have any focus left to watch the others, and it wasn't until Nasturtium let out a startled gasp that I finally glanced behind me.

"What?"

"My mother." She indicated the blank stretch of path in front of her. "She's gone."

"We reached the sage boundary," Ramsey said without any touch of an apology.

"You killed her!" Nasturtium said.

"Oh, get a grip," I said. "She was already dead and prob-ably only had as much power as she did because the Reaper was the one who brought her back."

Linnea herself walked in sullen silence, without a word to add, though I saw her eyes narrow when she spied several other officers approaching our group. Two of them moved to seize Nasturtium, and another two lifted my mother out of the air to carry her safely. Another helped take the Reaper off my brother's hands, though he continued to walk behind her as though he didn't trust her not to run.

"They aren't taking her to jail, are they?" I whispered. "What does one usually do with a rogue Reaper, even one who's in magical handcuffs?"

"Take her to the *real* Reapers," he said, ignoring the implied question in my words. "I already made a call."

"To whom?" My own phone buzzed, and I fished it out of my pocket. Maura. *About time.*

"Sorry," she said when I answered the phone. "I got held up. Is everything all right?"

"No." Not by a long shot. "No, but we trapped the rogue Reaper, and my brother's about to give me a full explanation about how he managed to pull it off."

Ramsey scowled at me. "Later."

"I'll hold you to that."

16

It was not all right. While Maura promised she'd come and banish the demon from the police station right away, Mum still hadn't woken up by the time we'd reached the house and the officers carried her inside at my request. I knew exactly what my mother would say to the notion of strangers entering the house when I hadn't redone the security spells yet, but I figured she wouldn't want to be taken to hospital, either.

When the officers had laid her in bed, Horace settled himself near Mum's head and curled protectively on the pillow.

*Now what?* I didn't want to leave Mum here without the security wards up, but the demon was still at the police station, and until Maura showed up, there'd be a risk of the monster escaping. Even with Linnea in handcuffs, waiting for whoever Ramsey had called in to arrest her.

"Aren't you going to let me in?" said a voice from outside Mum's bedroom door.

My heart missed a beat. "Is that…?"

*Grandma.* I ducked out of the room and spied her

hovering at the foot of the stairs. My mild horror at my grandmother's ghost being *inside* the house evaporated when she drifted upwards towards Mum's room.

"I'll keep an eye on her," Grandma told me. "No intruder will get past *me*."

"Erm," I said. "You're—"

"I know I'm a ghost," Grandma interjected. "I'm still capable of scaring off intruders, and if you put your security spells back on, no demon will be able to get inside."

There was supposed to be enough sage around the house to stop *her* from getting inside, but at a guess, Linnea had removed that too. I couldn't believe how easily she'd played us.

I gave in. "Fine. I need to make sure that Reaper doesn't slip away from my brother. Oh, and that nobody tries to arrest Maura."

I'd have to deal with the consequences of Grandma being able to enter the house later, but there was little else I could do for Mum at this point. Tansy and I left her with her ghostly guardian and made our way towards the main street.

By the time we reached the police station, Maura stood waiting outside. Several suspicious-looking officers hovered nearby—evidently, my brother hadn't let anyone go back into the station yet—and both Nasturtium and Linnea were in handcuffs.

"There you are," Maura said. "I was starting to think I'd be arrested next."

"Thanks for coming," I said to her. "I know it's not ideal, but we couldn't get rid of the demon on our own, so we had to put it in sage and hope for the best."

"I'll handle it." Her eyes narrowed at the other Reaper, who appeared to be sizing her up. "I hope you have someone reliable coming to deal with *her*."

The police station doors opened before us, revealing the

demon hovering within the circle of sage my brother had used to ensnare it.

"Back again?" asked the demon. "You couldn't find another Reaper willing to help you?"

Maura didn't so much as blink. "I can't imagine you'll be any more challenging to get rid of than the last time."

"That won't keep me out." The demon gave a cold laugh. "A reckoning is coming for you, Head Witch."

A slight commotion came from behind me, but I didn't dare take my eyes off the demon. "Just what is that supposed to mean?"

"You'll see." The demon surged forwards, and Maura shot out a hand.

Darkness engulfed the area, masking the demon and the sage circle, and when it had cleared, the demon was gone.

"Dammit." I swivelled to Maura. "I wanted to ask more questions."

"He wasn't going to give you the answers, Robin," she told me. "He was going to keep playing mind games until you finally released him by accident or otherwise."

I knew she was right, but on top of the Reaper's betrayal and Mum being in a coma, my nerves were fried. "My mother... Linnea did something to her. She had a hideout in the Wildwood, a kind of house, but it was *inside* the afterworld."

Maura's eyes widened. "She *is* a fully trained Reaper, then. I certainly can't do that."

"She trapped my mother in there, and when I got her out, she fell unconscious." I swallowed. "Do you know how long it'll take her to recover?"

Maura's brow furrowed. "I'm sorry. I've never dealt with that before, but if Linnea didn't kill her..."

"She'll have wanted her to survive to face her the next

time." Chills raced down my arms. "We'd better make sure my brother puts that Reaper somewhere secure."

When I left the police station, a group of strangers had Linnea surrounded. Two huge creatures with tusks—ogres— flanked her, escorting the false Reaper away from the police station.

Bewildered, I waylaid my brother. "Who are they?"

"The Wardens," said Ramsey. "They sometimes help with matters that would normally require the Reapers, and they're considerably easier to contact. They'll hand Linnea straight over to the council."

"Didn't you want to ask Linnea *why* she wanted revenge on our mother first?"

"She wouldn't say," he replied. "She blamed the coven, not its current leader, but there's bad blood there."

"I bet Grandma knows." My hands clenched into fists. "Again. You know, she's watching over Mum at home. We're never going to have a moment's peace again."

Maura cleared her throat from behind me. "I should go, but you should know I've worked with the Wardens before. They're trustworthy."

"Can they handle her, though?" I gestured to the ogres' retreating backs.

"If anyone outside of the Reapers can, it's them," she replied. "Anyway, my brother will be hopping mad that I ran off without telling him. Call me if you need me, all right?"

"I will." When she vanished, I turned back to my brother. "I hope she's right about the Wardens. When did you plan to tell *me* about your new contacts?"

"I didn't know if we'd need their help," he said, sounding apologetic. "Besides, the demons can read minds. Even yours."

I folded my arms across my chest. "But you told Mum."

"Actually, no."

"She'll be thrilled when she wakes up, then." My annoyance faded. We'd both been trying to accomplish the same goal, and there was no point in arguing. "The demon's gone. Maura took care of it."

"Good." He nodded to his fellow officers. "It's safe to go back inside. Take those two to the holding cells."

As I watched, the officers escorted Nasturtium and Radcliffe inside. "Are you sure you want to arrest them? Radcliffe… I mean, he's a squirrel."

"I'm aware," Ramsey said in weary tones, "but until I can arrange to have a curse-breaker come and remove the curse, we can't let him run around free."

"Right." I'd almost forgotten the curse in the wake of the general chaos, and it'd been Mum who'd been intending to call in the curse-breaker. Without her…

Tansy jumped onto my shoulder and curled her tail around my neck. "She'll wake up, Robin," she murmured into my ear, correctly guessing what I was thinking.

"I know." I squeezed my eyes shut. "I know she will."

---

Mum didn't wake up overnight. I'd suspected she wouldn't, but part of me had hoped that she'd be able to sleep it off. Like when I'd been in a coma myself, recovering from being held prisoner by a Reaper couldn't be accomplished by a single night of sleep. I'd recovered, but would she? A seed of doubt had sprouted in my heart, which only grew bigger when I went to see Dad. I'd called him the previous day—I hadn't wanted to keep him in the dark—but there was a limit to what I could say on the phone, and part of me had hoped Mum would wake up and assuage all my worries.

When she hadn't woken, I'd faced a dilemma over whether I should return to the office. Ramsey was back at work, of course, but I hadn't the mental fortitude to deal with Aunt Shannon's questions or the other council members' petty arguments. Instead, I instructed Chloe to tell the other witches that I was dealing with setting up the security wards around my family's property again, which was technically true, though I'd pretty much dealt with that the previous day after I'd returned home.

I'd also sprinkled sage around the entire house, which had kicked off a tantrum from my grandmother that I'd kind of hoped would be enough to wake my mother from her coma, but no luck. I had a sinking suspicion that Aunt Shannon had heard from next door, though, which was another reason I was loathe to show my face at the office until Mum woke up.

*Please, please wake up, Mum.*

Dad took the news of Mum's state well enough, though I had to refrain from sharing too many details while the kids were at home. Jessica was at work that day, leaving Dad in charge of the house, and he'd confessed his worries about the demon and the Reaper.

"The demon's long gone," I told him while Tansy distracted the boys by chasing them around the back garden. "Maura took care of him."

"But… the other Reaper," he said. "She was working against you?"

"I know," I said. "I don't get it either. Ramsey sent her off with the Wardens, so I'll have to hope they can handle her."

"And the other squirrel?" Dad watched Tansy run around the garden for a moment. "Was he helping the Reaper, or…?"

"Nope," I replied. "He was the one carrying the slug curse around, but he's not on the demons' side. Tansy thinks otherwise, but she's always had a thing about being the only red squirrel in town."

Nasturtium had been given a short prison sentence, as Ramsey had informed me when I'd asked, while Radcliffe had been spared on the grounds that she'd manipulated him. I wasn't sure if it was true, but a prison cell was incapable of containing the squirrel himself long term.

After the curse-breaker showed up, the squirrel would be freed from captivity, and I suspected he'd be happy to get out of Wildwood Heath and never come back.

"I bet," Dad said. "Speaking of the curse, how are your mother's flowerbeds?"

I winced. "I asked Piper to come around and fix them. I suppose the silver lining to this mess is that the garden will be back to normal by the time Mum wakes up."

"Your grandmother's watching her?"

"Yeah." I inclined my head. "Ramsey and I are taking shifts too. I'm technically supposed to be there while he's at work, but I figured she couldn't do anything too heinous in an hour."

"You'd better get home, then." He hugged me. "I'm sure your mother will be right as rain."

*I hope so.* Visiting Dad had put me in a slightly better mood, and I returned home in anticipation of another clash with Grandma. At least Araminta's ghost hadn't come back; she must have used up all the power the Reaper had given her when she'd led us to find Mum, or else her summoner's capture had drained her whatever was keeping her in the land of the living.

Grandma, by contrast, was as full of energy as ever and took to her new task of watching over Mum with the single-mindedness she'd usually applied to rearranging my office. Not that I trusted her alone, but Ramsey stepped in to watch Mum when evening rolled around so Harvey and I could go out to the Fox's Den together.

"Nice of him to offer," Harvey commented as we sat down at our usual table. "I'm surprised."

"I'm not," I said. "I've learned I can't predict anything with my family."

We fell into a companionable silence but not an uncomfortable one. I was just happy to be in his presence, away from the drama and strife.

At least until he spoke the words that nobody wants to hear on a date. "I have to talk to you."

My pulse surged, my heart racing in my chest. "About what?"

"I've had news," he said. "It's... Well, it's not the best timing, but I thought you should know. It's only fair."

"What is it?" My mind churned with possibilities, each more dire than the last. "Come on, tell me."

"It's good news," he said. "Our Sky Hopper team has qualified to compete on a national level, and we've been given a week to decide if we want to enter the preliminaries for next year's championships. That means we'll be playing all over the country."

The words buzzed in my skull. "You're... leaving?"

"Not forever," he said. "This is a once-in-a-lifetime chance, but I didn't want to leave when you're in such a dangerous situation."

"No, you have to go," I said. "It's your dream."

I'd thought I'd be the one leaving first, and despite reason telling me this would be temporary, with how precarious everything else in my life was... how could I know for sure?

He took my hand and squeezed. "This doesn't change anything."

*I hope it doesn't. I really do.*

---

With the security spells redone and no change in Mum's condition, I had no excuses left to avoid my return to the office the following day, and besides, I needed a distraction from the funk that Harvey's revelation had put me in. And from Grandma, who woke me up by rattling the windows every morning and tried to scare any non-family members who came near the house, including Kimberly and Piper.

"Please stop terrifying the staff," I told her over the break-fast table, after she'd sent our poor cook fleeing the room by turning the kettle off and on repeatedly.

Grandma bared her teeth in a grin. "Now, what's the point of having staff if you can't torment them a little?"

"Go and watch Mum instead." Honestly, it was kind of insulting that she seemed so cheery while my mother was in a magical coma with no signs of waking up. "I'm going to work."

I'd never have admitted it to Grandma, but the office felt unusually quiet when I showed up. Granted, Carmilla wasn't there, either; she'd followed Grandma when she'd relocated to my mother's house and had taken up her old habit of trying to trip me on my way out the door.

Chloe greeted me with a wan smile. "You didn't have to come back."

I shrugged. "Not much I can do at home."

"Lady Wildwood will wake up," she said. "She's made of strong stuff."

I took my seat. "I know, but what am I supposed to tell the council?"

"Ah." She ducked her head. "You should know there's a coven meeting today. Or we can reschedule..."

"Not again." I had to face them eventually. "They'll want answers, and I won't be fulfilling my role as Head Witch if I hide away."

The full story would have to wait until Mum woke up, but I could at least explain how we'd solved Araminta's murder and stopped the curse. As for the demon and the false Reaper... Okay, that would invite more questions that I'd struggle to answer, but over my dead body was I letting Aunt Shannon have the final word. Knowing her, she'd already told them about seeing the Reaper and the demon inside my mother's garden.

*I'll set the record straight myself.*

When the meeting time rolled around, I walked to the council room with Chloe. The murmur of voices already drifted out of the door, and when we walked in, we found almost every seat at the table occupied.

Aunt Shannon sat in Mum's usual seat. The sight sent a wave of fury washing over me. *Seriously?*

Walking to my seat, I cleared my throat. "Might I ask why the coven leader's seat is occupied?"

Aunt Shannon smiled benignly at me. "I've been appointed the temporary coven leader by a vote from the other council members."

*What?* "That's not allowed."

"I think you'll find it is if you read the rules." She smiled more widely. "I don't think you have, though, have you?"

*Mum never told me that was possible.* But why would she? She'd never thought her own position had been in jeopardy. "I'm Head Witch, not coven leader, but the council can't put anything to a vote without my say-so."

"On the contrary," she said, "when the Head Witch is believed to be incompetent, it's possible for the council to act independently."

"To do what?" I caught Chloe's eye and saw my own alarm reflected on her face. "I didn't see any of you come to help when we were under attack."

"Now, that's a little unfair," she said. "I was unaware that anything was happening at all, since the Head Witch saw fit to inform nobody outside of her own circle."

"There was no time. My mother's life was in danger." The

murmur of agreement that passed up and down the table made my fists clench, and I had the sinking suspicion that she'd been trying to win them over ever since I'd been taken out of commission. "Besides, I didn't want to incite a panic. If you'll allow me, I have a full explanation of the events to give."

"You'll have plenty of time during your trial."

*My* what?

Chloe spoke up. "You don't have the authority to put the Head Witch on trial."

"I beg to differ." Aunt Shannon nodded to the other gathering witches. "I've put together a committee to replace the Head Witch with someone more competent, and our first step will be a thorough interrogation to get to the bottom of this lapse in judgement."

"Lapse in judgement?" I held up the sceptre. "You want to accuse the *sceptre* of making the wrong choice? Also, do you really want both the Head Witch and the coven leader to be absent in a time of crisis?"

"When neither is currently fit to handle said crisis, I think it's for the best," she replied. "I've been researching thoroughly, and there have been cases like this in the past."

"Who do you think would be better? Yourself?" My voice rang out, shaking with fury despite my best efforts. She'd always wanted me to fail, but my brushing her off the other day must have put the final nail in the coffin. Add Mum being in a coma, and she'd known she wouldn't have a better chance than this.

"We'll see what the sceptre itself has to say." Aunt Shannon's gaze flickered to the glowing instrument in my shaking hands. "It's not unheard of for a sceptre to pick someone incompetent, and such matters are usually hushed up, but it *is* possible for the sceptre to be *encouraged* to pick someone else. The procedure is quite straightforward, if unorthodox."

Her words rocked me to the core. Not that she wanted to break with tradition—she'd throw anything aside if it aided her rise to power—but that the sceptre might have chosen someone else at any time. I wasn't tied to it. I never had been.

I'd wanted to retire as Head Witch, yes, but not like this. Not in a humiliating trial while my mother was incapacitated. Not after everything I'd fought for and everything I'd given up.

No. Aunt Shannon might have the support of the council, but I wasn't alone. I had my brother. I had my friends. And I had the contact details of a certain pair of reporters in my phone.

She wanted to play this game, did she? Fine. Bring it on.

# ABOUT THE AUTHOR

Elle Adams lives in the middle of England, where she spends most of her time reading an ever-growing mountain of books, planning her next adventure, or writing. Elle's books are humorous mysteries with a paranormal twist, packed with magical mayhem.

She also writes urban and contemporary fantasy novels as Emma L. Adams.

Visit http://www.elleadamsauthor.com/ to find out more about Elle's books.